Intention

Before

Healing

B

No one can heal the pain of another and no one has the responsibility for another's pain. We can be there,

we can support, we can listen but we cannot cure - that has to come from the bearer of the pain. No one else at all. Until that

H

pain is acepted, situations and people will arrive to remind, to exacerbate, to expose, to challenge, to annoy - until something is done by the bearer to

attempt a healing. When the honest intention of self-healing is there, then the universe sends in the listeners, the friends, the allowers. But not until the intention is there.

Philip J Bradbury

Men are understanding if you can understand them … if they can understand themselves. Men have served our civilization well – they have discovered new worlds, tilled the **45** soil, defended their people, **Moments** invented great machines, formulated **With** healing medicines, created beautiful **Men** and uplifting artworks, fathered gifted and happy children, inspired and soothed us with their songs and their writing, provided for and protected us in our daily lives. These things have not always been done the way you wanted, but they were done and they were done the best way men knew how. Most people on this planet are not evil and will do the best that they can, from their current level of understanding. You will look back on events of your life and know that if you had your life to live over again, you would do it differently, better. This is not to excuse the men of this world who have raped, destroyed, murdered, disempowered, abused and lessened in any way. They have **Philip J Bradbury** done these things and we must not walk away from that truth. They have, however, also done many great, inspiring, creative and loving things and we must not walk away from that truth. For whatever reason, the actions of men are generally more public than those of women – men are usually the more "out there" of the species and in times past, their achievements have been lauded loudly from high places. The time seems to have come when the balance is restored and when the evils of men are being lauded loudly from those high places. This is the time we are living in at the moment and it is, therefore, a time that many men are feeling very unwelcome and uncomfortable as participants in the human race. This is not altogether healthy for the growth of our Earth family, for we were created with two sides, two sexes, and one cannot grow without the other. Most of the stories are articles written for magazines. Some are about a real men (*Ordinary Adventures* and *The Old Git In The Corner*, for example) and the rest came out of my head, somehow. These stories are an attempt to help explain (not to excuse) the ways of men. In that understanding, I seek to help us all to grow in love and strength, and to all run this race, this human race, together. The other reason is that I just love writing stories.

Contents

The Birth of Stories   6
   To Dad   9
   The Men's Non-Movement   11
   More Bloody Words   14
   Boys Need Instructions   19
   Crushing Dreams   22
   The Old Git In The Corner   26
   The Wide Boys   29
   Getting Knotted   33
   The Soft Man   35
   Divorcing Our Parents   38
   Girls Can Do Anything … Almost   41
   Trial And Nearer   45
   I Am A Candle   49
   Shopping for Peace   50
   The Good Book   52
   Ordinary Adventures   58
   For Crying Out Loud   61
   Me Mate's Dead   64
   The Shy Boy   65
   We're All Addicts   68
   In And Out We Go   70
   MOTLOFOHIFS   73
   The Ancient Traveller   76

If you enjoyed this book enough to buy one for a friend - or yourself, your best friend - just scan this Quick Response (QR) Code with your smart phone and you'll be taken to my website at www.philipjbradbury.com

Womanly Ways	78
Where Are You Looking?	81
Fish And Ships In The Night	84
Who's Counseling Who?	88
Angry, Depressed Cars	91
Who Are You Really?	94
Speaking Without Words	97
Heart Of Nails	100
The Shyest Boy In The World	103
The Violence Within	106
Orgasms, Knowing And Belief	109
The Ages Of Man	112
Our Neolithic Roots	115
Finding My Feminine Side	118
Tough on the Outside	121
No Advice is No Vice	124
Where's Our Wild Men?	128
Shaming Men	131
Getting Out Of Love's Way	134
Reflecting On Life	137
The Hard Man	141
Little Bear	145
About the Author	153
Thank you ...	154
Other books by Philip J Bradbury	156

The Birth of Stories

It's 5.00 am, my writing hour, and I write the last story; the story of how the others arrived here.

Along with 520 other trainers, I was made redundant from careers Australia (CA), Australia's largest Registered Training Organisation (RTO). That was April 2016. Along with hundreds of other RTOs, CA had had to face up to the gross dishonesty they had foisted on thousands of naïve students and it was having to repay millions of dollars' worth of fees back to those earnest and hapless students.

Australia's education system is the most ineptly over-regulated one in the world and politicians, with egos larger than their hearts and minds, have all needed to "make a difference". And a difference they've made. Refusing to listen to those at the coal-face – the educators – they foisted the most insanely restrictive system that rewarded the fraudsters and penalised the honest. The way of remedying this has been to enforce more regulations which has had the interesting result of forcing the collapse of thousands of dishonest RTOs and raising a new breed of dishonest RTOs, leaving hundreds of thousands of students out of pocket and partly-completed qualifications, the government deeper in debt and thousands of educators out of work.

After the redundancy I did some part-time work for two RTOs (Australian Technology and Trade College and Australis College) who had me sign their 20-page employment contracts, perform the work and then ignore their own contracts – and Australian law – by refusing to pay me. I did some work for a more honest RTO (Diversity Training) but their honesty and naivety saw them sinking beneath the weight of bureaucracy and government ineptitude … and the lies of a very slick salesman. They could only pay a fraction of what I was owed and I finally realised my time as a teacher in Australia was over, like so many of my ex-colleagues.It was time to look elsewhere.

I could have gone back to accounting, the career I hated for 20 years and the one that got me into the career I loved for 20 years – teaching. But my heart and soul could not go back and my wife wouldn't allow me to. I became so unhappy and unpleasant when I did what I hated, she preferred starvation to that!

Where else to look?

Aha, the activity I love most – writing. I spent a week travelling round my computer and found 296 short stories. And, in the meantime, I continued to write more. Many were from the once-upon-a-time, distant past and I'd forgotten I'd written them ... or remembered them but forgotten what they were about.

I read them and found I still loved reading them – the cynical, the emotional, the humorous, the instructional, the fanciful, the lyrical and the deeply moving. I loved them all.

The sorting task has two sticking points, though.

Firstly, it was not the simple one-of-two-choices type of selection for there was such a variety of tales and types of tales. The task of sorting them into six books was not the task of sorting our rubbish – recycling or not recycling – or the task of sorting our washing into whites or non-whites. It took some time to invent six different categories and, even then, many stories could go into two or more of the artificial categories I'd created.

The second limiting factor was that these tales were my babies. Over 22 years of writing, I'd given birth to these 296 stories – and 20 partly-finished ones, as well as twelve non-fiction books and novels – and I found it emotionally draining to read each one.

There are milestones in our lives and we're brought back to them with the playing of old songs, the hearing of familiar phrases, the wafting of pungent smells, the meeting of old friends and the reading of old stories. I was stilled, time and again, as each narrative rebirthed an old memory, an old regret, an old success, an old failure, an old joy.

But I ploughed on and eventually had six categories:

Fables

Men

Self

God

Writing

Poems/songs

But then, you see, I had run a writing group in Brisbane and currently run two and attend another in Ipswich. These writing groups encourage the spawning of at least a story a week. I had to draw the line and tell the recent stories they must wait for the next train, the next book. I hated to leave some out – it seemed so unfair to them – but books don't become published via the medium of procrastination and soft-heartedness.

So, today's the day – 28th October 2016 – and the books go to press, one by one. Firstly, it's this book, *43 Moments With Men* and, next, it's *53 Moments With Fables*. A random decision, sure, but one has to make black-and-white decisions in a rainbow world.

These are my babies, my children, now grown to adults as I send them out into the world to you and other readers.

I hope they give you as many smiles, tears, sighs, insights and joys as they've given me.

To Dad

First intro: A7   D7   G7

C   G   C   C7
Here I stand, a man - alive and free,
F   C
I've beaten odds and I will again, many times.
F   C
I've had my ups and downs, smiles and tears,
C   G   C
But I've more of me than I had before.

Now I'm asking for more of you, the inside.
I want to know your truth, your "behind the scenes" story,
What makes you tick, what gives you smiles and tears.
Pull back the curtain and let me see inside.

First intro

There you stand, a man - alive and free,
You've won at life and you will again, many times.
You've had your jobs, your dogs, your smiles and tears,
But there's also me, perhaps your best achievement yet.

Please acknowledge that success, that me,
The one who wants a hug, a smile, a gentle "yes",
Let us teach each other and share the smiles and tears,
And say "well done" and laugh at the not-so-well-done.

Chord change intro: B7   E7   F7

D   A   DD7
Here we stand, two men - alive and free,
G   D
Free to be sad, lacking, fearful and down,
G   D
Alive enough to hug, alive enough for smiles and tears,
            A   D
We'll each say "I love you" and know it's for keeps.

My love for you is never dead, you don't escape,
You can be mean and ugly, silly and dumb,
I'll love you forever, through smiles and tears,
And in that space I'll love me and you'll love you.

Chord change intro

More than we can ever know. G   C

The Men's Non-Movement

The Women's Liberation Movement burst into our living-rooms some thirty years ago with a strident, demanding, angry, divisive and separatist energy. And that's as it should be for it was about women reclaiming their masculine (yang) energy. While it is recognised that the public persona of the Movement was probably the tip of the iceberg, with most women just asserting themselves in a quiet (and often unsupported) way, it came across as a Women's Movement with masculine energy.

Ask people today about the Men's Movement and most don't know it exists. Of those who do, few have any idea of what it's really about. That, too, is as it should be for it's about men reclaiming their feminine (yin) sides and it is more about the inside things - feelings, acceptance of themselves and being able to communicate better on an emotional level. The Women's Movement was more about the outside things - recognition and acceptance from others.

The Women's Movement was just that - a desire to move physically from one place of work or being to another. The men's one is really a Non-Movement - it's about standing still (perhaps, for a change) and learning to love and accept the wholeness, the fullness, within.

Because it's about inside things, it asks nothing of anyone else. We have a Ministry of Women's Affairs, a Ministry of Maori Affairs, a Ministry of Foreign Affairs and a Ministry of Youth Affairs. So where does a thirty plus, paler, New Zealand male go to for his Affairs? It is this group, unrecognised by authorities, that generally makes up the Men's Non-Movement, although it is starting to be joined by many not born in this country. There will never be a Ministry of Men's Affairs if the Men's Non-Movement has its way, for the recognition and acceptance that comes from within is all that is needed, as the women in the submerged part of their "iceberg" probably found.

Because of that, the changes seen on the outside of men are very subtle, while the women burned their bras, dressed in men's clothing (stark black and white suits, sometimes with a tie) and acted more assertively. It is interesting to note that while a woman in men's clothes is now accepted, a man is ousted from the Police Force (male organisation) for wearing women's clothes. However, the men say nothing about this for the power they feel within comes about from acceptance and a certainty about the "quiet way", rather than a demanding of some wrong to be righted.

As Steve Biddulph says in *Manhood*, "Men are hurting. They are also hurting others". And he later says, "Women's enemies were largely in the world around them. Men's enemies are often inside - in the walls we put up around our own hearts. The inner changes will have to come before we can heal the world. Coming out from behind these walls (slowly, carefully) will mean that men can change and grow - to our own benefit and to the benefit of women and children".

The answers, we see, can only come from within and when that never-ending process is underway, the "answers" will come for the rest of society. Steve lists some Australian facts:

- Men, on average, live for six years less than women,
- Men routinely fail at close relationships. (Just two indicators: 40% of marriages break down, and divorces are initiated by the woman in four out of five cases.)
- Over 90% of convicted acts of violence will be carried out by men, and 70% of the victims will be men.
- In school, around 90% of children with behaviour problems are boys and over 80% of children with learning problems are boys.
- One in seven boys will experience sexual assault by an adult or an older child before the age of eighteen.
- Men comprise over 90% of inmates of gaols. Men are also 74% of the unemployed.
- The leading cause of death amongst men between twelve and sixty is self-inflicted death. In the 1993 ABS statistics, suicide accounted for one in every 38 male deaths overall.

New Zealand has the world's highest rate of male teenage suicide and the unemployment, crime and prison statistics are similar.

Because of the low-key and unstructured nature of this Non-Movement, the numbers involved are unknown. However, as an indicator, Chris Angus, who has run the Tauranga Living without Violence programme for the last ten years, says he is approached by about 250 men per year, of which 70% actually do the programme. He runs six programmes per week, fifty one weeks a year, and similar programmes are run in most New Zealand towns and cities.

Rex McCann (one of New Zealand's leading facilitators of men's workshops) has run over a hundred of his *Essentially Men* courses around the country, since 1990. Along with several other courses, he has touched and enriched the lives of thousands of men. The *Essentially Men* course is a weekend workshop to take men through the gateway of knowing and loving themselves in a very powerful and gentle way. This is followed by smaller groups then meeting (usually) two weekly to support and encourage the positive changes.

When I attended the *Essentially Men* workshop I was surprised at the incredibly strong feelings of abandonment, abuse and even hatred expressed, by some, towards their parents, especially fathers. I was glad I was not the pillows and mattresses that took the force of those expressed emotions but, at the end of it, all those men wanted to do was to hug their fathers or mothers and to say they loved them. This, to me, is the essence of this Non-Movement – the negativity felt inside is faced squarely and dealt with, with no-one else being blamed or hurt. Out of this comes the aspiration to communicate more positively and effectively with others. Self-responsibility is paramount.

The answer, we know, can come from no-one but ourselves. To quote Neale Donald Walsch's *Conversations with God*, "if we don't go within, we go without". And so the way of the Men's Non-Movement is the quiet way, the gentle way, the way of self-responsibility – the way of real strength.

More Bloody Words

Tony wasn't the biggest boy in class but he soon realized that winning was not about size but action and intent - if you went in first, with enough fury and gestures and with absolute certainty of winning, the fight was yours. And so a fighter he became, with every success proving (yet again) his was the only way.

Peter, a bigger and stronger boy, had a different inclination and tended to win his fights by a hundred yards. Aggression and violence repelled his very being, his stomach churned and his legs took him from the arena before he knew what was happening.

The story of how these two boys came to understand each other's approach is interesting but that they swapped roles for a time is more intriguing. It probably started when they had to recite poetry in class and Peter chose his favourite poet, Spinafex John, a gentle and philosophic man. One phrase stuck in Tony's mind and annoyed the hell out of him:

In the quiet waiting-room of your mind,
There's none to see but your own gentle self.

Why it annoyed him so much he couldn't tell but, somehow, that type of crap got right up his nose. At lunch time he confronted Peter with it:

"What the hell is that sort of stuff supposed to mean? All those words telling you nothing about nuttin'."

"Well … I liked them," stammered Peter, anticipating a blow from some direction.

"I didn't. They're just a pile of horse-shit, saying nothing," said Tony, plumping himself down beside Peter. "Why don't they write about real things? You know, stories about things that really happen."

"The Waiting Room is a kind of story, a story about what happens in our mind," said Peter, surreptitiously packing up his lunch and looking for an exit path. "It's a story that belongs to everyone if you want to look into the depth of the words."

"'Depth of the words', what crap!" asserted Tony. "You don't 'look into words'. They tell you things, things that are more bloody useful than your rubbish."

"Yes, I suppose some words do tell a story", mused Peter. "But some don't - they simply open your mind for you to discover your own story." He wasn't quite sure what he was saying, this 14 year old boy, but his own words felt comforting. And right, somehow.

"And what the hell's that all supposed to mean?" demanded Tony. "All this 'discover your own story' stuff? You're as bad as your poet - pretty phrases telling you bull-shit nothing!"

"I guess if you can't feel the words, if they have no meaning for you, then they don't," said Peter, feeling strangely more relaxed as Tony's tension grew. "If they mean nothing, then let them go - they aren't for you."

"What do you mean 'let them go'! I can't get the silly buggers out of my head now!" blurted Tony. "Once they're in there, they fly round like a bloody egg-beater. What'd you have to say them for anyway?"

"Because I liked them," explained Peter. "And I thought some others might like them too."

"Well I didn't and they're annoying the hell out of me!" said Tony, beating a fist into a palm.

"Well let them go then."

"I bloody can't," exploded Tony, leaping up. "You bloody stuck them in here and you can bloody well get them out!"

Peter was stunned to silence and others quickly moved away. This aggressive stance could only mean one outcome.

"Well, what are you going to do?" Tony demanded.

"I ... well ... I'm not sure what I can do," pleaded Peter. I don't know how to take words out of people's heads."

"You'd better think of something pretty quick or you're for it!"

"Perhaps we could …"

"Not we. You," retorted Tony. "You started this."

A moment of silence followed, a moment Peter felt was large

enough to be filled by his entire life but which may not have been longer than the tick of a clock. In this desperate moment, a knowing filled his entire being and he instantly knew there was an alternative to running, an alternative he hadn't conceived of before.

"Tony," he said with a new voice that came from his belly, "I thought you were a fighter. And now you want me to do your fighting for you."

Tony's upraised hand froze in mid-air and his silence was almost audible.

"You'll fight anyone, big or small, yet you can't face a battle with a few little words."

"What ... what are you saying?" asked Tony meekly.

"I'm not sure," said Peter. "I'm just puzzled how quickly your fighting spirit departs. This poetry must seem to be an immense opponent. Perhaps we can tackle this together."

"I don't need any bloody help!"

"Great!" said Peter. "Your fighting spirit is back!"

"But how do I get them out of my head?" asked Tony, slumping down on the seat beside Peter.

"I'm not quite sure," said Peter. "Perhaps you first need to ask yourself if the words are really for you in some way. If they weren't they mightn't bug you so much."

"Maybe," mumbled Tony, after a moment's silence.

"Maybe," repeated Peter. "Is that a 'yes' or a 'no'?"

"Maybe, maybe not."

"Let's just pretend that your maybe is a 'yes'. If so, why would that be?" asked Peter.

"All this silly 'peace of mind' stuff," said Tony, quietly. "It's not real ... it's not possible."

"Spinafex John had it, I have it sometimes, so why not you?"

"You can't, you just can't be that happy. Everyone's worried about something," said Tony.

"Yes, I get worried about things, but things don't worry me," said Peter, a little mystified by his own words.

"More stupid words meaning nuttin'," said Tony, exasperated. "Can't you say something helpful?"

Not quite understanding the meaning of his previous words, Peter was, momentarily, stumped for a reply. Then, out of the mist of his knowingness, a string of words appeared: "Any worry I feel comes from inside, not from things or people outside. It's quite nice, really, for I can control inside things - outside things I can't."

"But I only get angry when other people are stupid," explained Tony.

"Maybe, maybe not."

"What are you saying?" asked Tony, feeling something stirring inside.

"Maybe your anger is really like mine and comes from inside," suggested Peter. "Maybe you're already angry inside and you only feel it when someone else pulls it out …"

Tony was stunned to silence.

Peter wasn't sure what to say next but wanted to put Tony at ease: "If you know you can start your own anger or worry then you also know you can stop it. Other people are really helpful in showing us what's really inside and I thank them for that."

There was a moment's silence while Tony felt a new sensation slowly rising up inside - a sensation he could only describe as peace. Tears tried to creep out and he squeezed his eyes tightly shut. The tears stayed inside but from the darkness appeared a small yellow light which slowly grew and grew, till most of the blackness was gone. He hadn't seen this yellow before but it looked quite nice - sort of like the peace feeling he had in his tummy. He kept his eyes closed for a moment longer, while the pressure from his tears died down, and then opened them with a small feeling of regret.

"It's actually quite nice in there," he said, a little embarrassed at the words he uttered.

"The light's always in there," said Peter. "We just choose to black it out for some reason."

"Probably fear," said Tony quickly, surprising himself with his words. Then he wondered how Peter knew what he had seen.

"Probably because it's what I've seen so many times."

Just then the bell rang and, with a sigh of relief, Tony leapt up to go - he'd had about as much of this soft stuff as he could stand. He did wait, though, for Peter to get up. As they walked back to the classroom, Tony realized his arm was around Peter's shoulders. He said "thanks", as a tear escaped from his eye.

"So what are you doing after school?" asked Tony.

"Probably walking home with you," said Peter, with a smile.

More tears leaked from Tony's eyes as they walked into the classroom. Everyone wondered how soft Peter could bring the school bully to tears and he became a bit of a hero. For the first time in his life, Tony couldn't give a damn. And it felt good.

Boys Need Instructions

The Lakota symbol for man is two spears pointing skywards, representing two warriors standing back to back, defending the village. We like to care and we like to do stuff.

A few years after my eighteen-year marriage was over, I discovered what to do with a clitoris; an exasperated woman gave me lessons on how she wanted to be treated. Till then, it had been a total mystery to me.

It was many years after that, in a men's group, that I finally admitted my shameful ignorance. The reaction was one of shared relief and laughter – most of the other men carried that same shameful ignorance and it was amazing to realise I wasn't the only idiot. Very few men had been told what women liked. In fact, most of us had been repeatedly told what women didn't like and that included our revolting bodies and useless love-making techniques.

Admittedly, few of us had sat a woman down and told her what we liked – few of us knew this ourselves. Those few who had had the parental sex chat had found it sordidly lacking in helpful information about what we could/should do and boringly filled with stuff we could do nothing about – how babies grew, how they were born, menstruation and so on.

Men, you see, are the fixers of the world. We like to do stuff. We like to fix stuff. We like to renovate houses, invent technology, train dogs and horses, drive faster and further. We like to explore the unexplored and we're always willing to hear of a more efficient, effective or enjoyable way to do things. We don't mind being told what to do if there's a tangible benefit for someone … anyone. The benefit doesn't have to be for us. In fact, we're happy to put ourselves second in order to benefit someone else.

The important word here is DO – it's only two letters but it's a HUGE word for us. We love doing things – moving our hands, feet, elbows, penises, anything.

Then this Martian-minded creature comes along and tells us to explore our feelings. What do we move there? Nothing! That's like asking a fish to climb a tree – just no possibility or comprehension.

Ask a man what he feels and he'll look at you blankly. No, he's not being obstinate, annoying or stupid. He's not hiding anything for he has nothing to hide. He's being starkly truthful. He doesn't know.

He knows is that's a 3 millimetre, reverse-threaded hex screw and all a woman knows it's a little shiny thing.

She knows whether it's a feeling of sadness or of loss and all a man knows is that it doesn't feel good.

The nuances of feelings arrive in the package when women are born and, because of their awareness of these nuances, they have a vocabulary for them. In the same way, a dog can identify a hundred different smells in a five-minute walk and a human can't. A thirteen-year old girl's emotional vocabulary usually exceeds a thirty-year old man's.

You see, men write instruction manuals and some of us even read them. We like to know what to do next.

In Indigenous and older cultures, the older men take the younger men aside and initiate them – they instruct them in the ways of the clan or tribe. They give them instructions and then send them out to test their learning in dangerous and unsafe ways. Dangerous and unsafe are magnets for men. If they're successful, they're praised and awarded, usually in painfully memorable ways.

Men and women are different with pain too!

Women hurt on the outside but not on the inside. Men are the opposite. We get man flu' and we're dying. But we break a collar bone and continue playing rugby. We smash a hand with a hammer and it hurts … but that hurt isn't a problem. So, when women tell us not to do something because it will hurt, we wonder what the problem is. We skin our knees, brush the gravel and carry on. Pain on the outside is simply pain. It's not a problem.

So, now we have two problems: lack of men and lack of pain.

With the shifting sands of relationships and marriages, many men do not grow up with men. They're raised by a single mother and schooled by female teachers and constantly told to be careful, don't do this or it will hurt, don't do that for it's unsafe. What? Don't do something because it's unsafe? That's the best reason for doing anything, mother!

They're held back from experiencing their world, physically, and they eventually break out, vying for the attention of older men. Most of these older man are authority figures – police, headmasters, bosses – who are great magnets for young men. They commit crimes just to be noticed and, also, because they've been denied their natural inclination for the dangerous and unsafe till now.

With a lack of strong and authentic males to model, they model the dysfunctional politicians, sportsmen and actors they see acting up on television and in movies.

It's not women's fault – they just naturally assume men know what women do and think like women do.

Men need challenges. They need pain, danger and unsafe. And even the most intelligent – I had six qualifications at the time – need instructions and a tangible benefit. The benefit of a happy woman is one of the best we can imagine. Like I said, we like to care and we like to do stuff.

Crushing Dreams

S queezed between their unmoving expectations and his fluid dreams, like the cars in the car crusher he operated for his father on weekends, Justin was constantly out of breath and out of confidence.

His father, his holey singlet over his beer gut, in shorts and sockless boots, strides round his scrap metal yard like a commander in battle, fighting for every penny and vestige of control. The control Bert had over his wife, now beyond reach, has now been laid on Justin double time. This dusty gravel yard of rusting, sharp and dead vehicles "was going to be all his" at some indeterminate time "when he finally grew up and manned up". That was his father's unwavering plan and Justin should be damned well grateful for it.

Justin's mother, Tina, was the eternally obedient wife till the last slap and punch smashed her lamp of timidity and out stepped the genie of quiet confidence. She started clandestinely reading self-help books and then pretended to be visiting her sister while actually attending a two-day motivational seminar. That motivated her out of her marriage. Shaking and crying, she packed her suitcase while Bert negotiated the sale of a broken Holden with a group of petrol heads, and walked out with no idea of where to go. She slumped down in a café she'd passed a zillion times on errands for Bert, a café she'd always dreamed of relaxing in like ordinary folk do … actually, any café would have done … as she just wanted to feel what it was like to relax and smile like an ordinary person, immersed in that coffee aroma, that orgasm for the nostrils, and do absolutely nothing but sit and watch people. She handed over half of the money she'd been able to steal from Bert and bought a latte – the name sounded so deliciously foreign – and a muffin and sat, looking round like a nervous magpie.

The waitress noticed Tina's distress and bruises and asked her where she was headed. Tina didn't know and ended up at the local women's refuge. A year later she had established a life in the next town – the genie of confidence had grown but not enough to let go of her roots too far – a nice, rented apartment, a part-time job as a bookkeeper and a ferocious desire to have her son back. Her publicly-funded lawyer had secured his release for every second weekend and her incandescent need for him and for his personal freedom was as smothering as was his father's control.

Justin knew he was supposed to love his parents – it's what everyone does, right? – and he felt he was missing an emotional gene or two because he really didn't like either of them. He tried to be normal and nice and he managed to fool everyone but himself.

His mother's verbal beatings – live your passion, find your bliss, do what fires your heart – could not be argued with. He fervently wished he could follow his passion, as all her books screamed at him, but he didn't have one. He fervently knew what he didn't want – the life others were designing for him – but he had no idea what he did want.

And he was so lonely. The boys around him at his father's place were fired up about driving fast, drinking lots and kicking dogs and footballs. He really tried to join in but no one was convinced. His father would scream at him and whack him when he declined their fishing and shooting trips and chose not to drive about whistling at girls and swearing at the homeless. None of it fitted him.

He fitted more with his mother's crowd but, even there, they seemed to be just a little too fragile and excited, as if they were about to fall from the cliff of life, clinging to it with happy positivity and magic phrases that were meant to make it all better. Yes, his mother's life had improved but both his parents seemed to have become more desperate – his father for control and his mother for freedom. Neither had much of either.

His dreams, if he ever had any, were to curl up in a cave, leave the feverish, panic-stricken world behind and play. It would have been nice to share his cave with someone else but he knew there was no one as weird and dysfunctional as himself. His computer games were his best refuge, at the moment, and he designed whole Simpson communities on the screen; places of deep serenity and solid contentment. Places where acceptance of that which was abounded, places where smiles were smaller and more natural and jokes never hurt anyone. Places where weird ones like himself could enjoy listening to each other and to nature. Places that seethed with respect and hummed with contentment. Places like that. It kept him busy for hours, much to his parents' annoyance. Both of them berated him to "get out into the real world; experience it and don't waste your time running away from it".

The more they told him not to run away, the more he wanted to, as if their advice was something that was supposed to help. Actually, it just hurt.

Trapped in everyone else's crusher with expectations blowing past him like the changeable weather, he became the master of disguise, camouflaging his behaviour to slip by, unnoticed, in any crowd. He learned the phrases, poses and pretences of every group and could pass as a rugby hooligan or a motivational guru; an arrogant sexist or a sensitive male; or even a really nice young man.

He learned to bottle up his anger, frustration, caring and his passions. He learned, without conscious awareness, to bottle himself up.

It was only a little thing his mother criticized him for but it struck a hundred short fuses and, before he knew what happened, she was sprawled on the floor, her lip bleeding.

She reacted not from that but from Bert's abuse, many years before and called the police. Bert reacted from his guilt, from many years before. He yelled that Justin was out of the house and disowned.

The sentence was light but, without a home, he was sent to a correctional facility and then to foster parents. The vacuum was eerie for a time for they had no plans for him, no expectations beyond wanting him to find his own peace. Peace? What the heck was that?

With no boundaries, he found it was okay to be angry, sad, lost, crying and distant. They seemed to understand that anything bottled up needed to be released. His bottle didn't smash, as his mother's had, but it dissolved in the sweet waters of acceptance, from the top down.

As the anger and tears dissipated he found, at the bottom of his bottle, an urge, a passion, for buildings and communities.

His foster parents adopted him and helped him through university. He emerged as an environmental architect and, though he'd wanted to, decided not to change the world. He decided just to change his little world.

By now his father had damaged his own body beyond repair with alcohol, nicotine and anger and his third heart attack brought an end to an era.

Surprised beyond belief, Justin found he had inherited the largest wrecking yard in the state and had no hesitation in giving away the dead and tortured bodies to clear a space for his eco-village.

Setting it up and running it was not all sweetness and light. He, of all people, knew the needs of people to assert their control and freedom over others. He quietly persisted and succeeded.

The one remnant of his father's that he kept was the crushing machine, which he mounted on a plinth to remind himself and others just how easily we can be twisted and squashed by the power of others' worst fears. He added a plaque to it: "Have a crush on life and not be a crush under life."

The Old Git In The Corner

From the old git in the corner, with nothing useful to say – so they told him – I learned more about life and myself than all the squawking young crows around us.

It was the first time I'd played my saxophone in public. My music teacher had teamed me up with friends of his and we were to play at a Maori wedding in my home town of Martinborough; population 400. I was nervous. No, I wasn't nervous. I was petrified. So the others in the band took me to the pub to "wash away the nerves", as they termed it. At fourteen, I wasn't allowed in the pub but, well, I was a local and it was Martinborough – a friendly cop and I was with older men. What harm could come of it?

I drank way too much for my first time drinking and then played up a storm. A real Charlie Parker, wowing the band and wedding guests alike … apparently. I don't remember much of it and woke the next morning with a fuzzy head and little idea how I'd found myself in this strange bed.

I stumbled into the kitchen, trying to focus my eyes, and was hit by the happy sounds of half a dozen people all cooking up; the smell of bacon, eggs, baked beans, toast and coffee filled my delicate nostrils and I sought somewhere to sit and ease my knotted stomach.

Then I spied him at the far end of the room. There was a bench seat round two walls, behind the kitchen table, and he'd been shoved in the corner and told to get on with his breakfast and shut up. In the storm of activity, I saw him as a still place to be. There was something else about him that drew me but I knew not what. I slid in beside him and smiled. He smiled back uncertainly.

Yes, he did have that old man smell, like wet wool and old socks. Yes, his shaving was haphazard with patches of whisker round his chin and down his neck. Yes, he did mumble and dribble his milk. But something drew me to him.

Some irk had filled his tea-cup to the top and I could see his hands were shaking a little. I grabbed his cup and drank it down a bit. He smiled and nodded a thank you.

I asked him what he'd done in his life and his eyes quickly filled, like a spa suddenly unleashed. He stared at me for a full minute and it took me longer than that to realise it was the first time anyone had asked him about himself. The first time in a very long time.

His speech was a bit blurred on account of his ill-fitting dentures and I had to ask him to repeat himself several times. He didn't seem to mind because, perhaps, someone was listening. Really listening. So he told me his story.

In 1899, at the age of fourteen, he'd been shanghaied from the streets of London and forced to work on a sailing ship. He never saw his parents again and endured dreadful discipline. However, a survivor just gets on with it and, after two years, had sailed round the world – America, Australia, South Africa, Spain, Morocco, India, Fiji … he'd been everywhere. Uncomplaining, he'd risen in the ranks but never lost his hatred for his captain and, the first chance he got, he jumped ship in San Francisco. He'd joined the Fairbanks Gold Rush in Canada and made little money but survived by trapping and making clothes for the miners, having learned to sew on the sailing ship. He then followed the Cobalt Silver Rush in Canada, mining furs, not minerals, and then tired of being frozen all the time.

He found his way to New York, working in a railway gang and casual farm work and paid his passage on the first ship he saw in the harbour. It happened to be going to Australia and he didn't care. He just wanted to keep running.

He mined for gold in Australia for six months and lost all his savings so set out for Melbourne to find a more prosperous land. He ended up in India, working in a tea plantation. He worked his way up to become the manager of the plantation for over twenty years. He happened to meet a young lass there – a lass from New Zealand – and followed her back home to marry her and spent the rest of his life building boats in

Wellington.

They then retired in Martinborough, bringing up four strapping boys who fathered some of the cackling crows in the kitchen. They loved the old bugger but no one had ever heard his story … till I was prompted to listen.

He'd gone out mining for gold and silver and I was the one who found the most precious metal of all – the beautiful story of a beautiful old man who no one ever listened to.

The Wide Boys

The Wide Boys they were. Not sure why we called them that. No one knows for sure. Seems like the name just oozed out of the mud and we adopted it; gave it to them and it stuck.

So, that's them, the Wide Boys – Sonny, Sammy and Boris. Always in that order. Always Sonny, Sammy and Boris.

Always Sonny out in front; smile as big as the sun, absolutely topper togs – ever the best from Joe Millers Menswear – and shoes with the shine of a new dollar, despite the muck thy sometimes trod in. Word was he wasn't baptised Sonny. It was probably Brian or Justin or some clodhopping name. So, not sure why Sonny but perhaps he thought he was the Son of God or something. Never quite sure.

Then, a little behind like a depleted Roman phalanx were Sammy and Boris, one on each side. Always about to overtake Sonny but never quite making it. Sammy was Christened Samuel – good Jewish stock

– and Boris … well, he was no Russian at all. Just another Bronx Jew with a yearning to outgrow his roots, outgrow the myriad rules that imprisoned us. Like most of us, really.

Sonny was the face of the Wide Boys, the talker, the arranger, the big vision guy with the cheek of a pirate's parrot. There was nothing he couldn't sort for you, source for you. You asked, you paid, you received. His nails were clean as a baby's thoughts and mud never stuck to the shine of his promise.

Sammy's nails, my friend, often carried the green of the dollar. If it was money you wanted, folding cash, he was your man. Greenbacks sprouted from his orchard – or the printing press no one saw – like figs on a summer's day. You could write a cheque for dosh you didn't have and, with a nod and a wink – and a back-hander, of course – your cheque would smile its way to the bank.

Now Boris, my friend, was a different bag of monkeys. His fingernails had neither shine nor green. They mighta' had a bleaker hue, like blood and mud and the smell of pain all mixed in. If you needed someone to quieten down – short or long term – a buck or two would have it done. You wouldn't, of course, ask him the favour. It would go through Sonny. But it'd be Boris who'd be gone for an hour or a day and then return with his grim smile and skinned knuckles.

So the Wide Boys were set for success, for stardom. Nothing in their way. Well, none's we could see. But it seems there's always something in all our ways. And the bigger our ways, the smaller the stone trips us up. The higher we fly, the thinner the cord to cut, if you know me meanin'.

See, they never worked. Well, not like us boot clodders, hauling sacks, driving machines, shovelling coal and the like. We all turned up for work on the dot, obeyed the man, sweated and cursed in the mud, dust and noise and could just afford enough for a nightly beer and a crappy wee rental for our lives.

Meanwhile, the Wide Boys drank their coffee on the pavement by day at the swankiest cafés and their cocktails at night at the swankiest clubs. Just sitting round chatting and suiting themselves to the hours they sauntered.

We's all pretty thankful for their favours, from time to time, though they'd cost our last few pennies and our next few dollars, I can tell you. We all had troubles that needed fixing and they were the blokes to fix them. No one wanted them gone … well, so we thought.

See, some guys can get real cranky that others have the smooth while they bear the rough, while some wear the white silk shirts while they wear the dirt-brown overalls. Jealousy's a funny thing as it's got no logic or perspective, no long-term plan. Looking the opposite way to Truth, it makes up its twisted story and no other will do, despite the evidence. The story twists the man and he twists his friends and, pretty soon, there's an anger and injustice that's fuelled by none but a fantasy. But, you see, injustice must have justice and anger must have an outlet, no matter how insanely triggered.

So these stories started up and not by anyone any of us know. They just seemed to float from the sky and the dusty sweat in their eyes blinded some fellas to the thought they might not be true. Maybe there's people just looking for a fight. When you look for blame, you'll find it easy enough. There's always someone to throw a hammer at when you're fired up against yourself, against your failure and your shitty life. When we're twisted up against our own fate, we never see our own part in it; we only look for and find – too easily – some other critter who forced you down.

I can't be sure but that's as how I imagined it happen. One bloke twists a story, just a tweak, the next one tweaks some more and in no time angels are devils, white is black and the innocent are hanged. Well, not literally. No one actually got hanged but near as dammit.

When the ruckus died down and we had time to reflect on it after a few jars of ale, the consensus was it started that day, a warm New York summer's day. See, Sally-Ann was the girl Big Herb was sweet on and he imagined she was sweet on him. We all thought so too but who'd ever know what's on another's mind. The thing was, Big Herb had confided he was going to propose to her but felt ashamed for his lack of finances. We told him to ask anyway for not asking had the same result of her saying no.

So, there he was, all hot under the collar, nervous and jumpy, and about to ask her the Big Question that coming Friday. Then someone saw her with the boys, Sonny and Sammy – supping coffee outside Bruno's Café. Then the story got made, got twisted, brains went awry and plans got made.

Of course, the Wide Boys weren't just three. They had eyes and ears everywhere and, soon enough, Big Herb found himself alone at night, face to face with Boris. The inevitable happened and Big Herb was seen no more. Concrete feet on the ocean floor was the most persistent rumour.

Trouble was, Big Herb had kicked up such a racket about it the preceding week. So everyone knew trouble was brewing, including Big Herb's father, Len, the factory's union boss. While unions pretend to hate employers, there's sneaky back-handers and secret friendships so Len called up some favours from the bosses, in a quiet friendly way and they … well, the story goes … leant on some cafés and clubs that mighta' been … not saying they were … mighta' been fronts for more clandestine operations. Then the Wide Boys' operations got strangled a bit and their promises went unkept and some, of course, were to the cops in this dirty, twisted town.

So the printing presses and whisky stills that weren't ever seen suddenly got seen. Boris was mighty handy with his fists on a well-planned night but, this time, surprised by eight pairs of fists and tools, he stood no chance. So now Sonny is all exposed, without protection and the cops have to do something as they're exposed too. They need someone to pass their dirty little lies to and so into the clink go Sonny and Sammy, quick smart and everyone's happy. And they didn't ever come out of that place because some twisted stories and twisted brains found reason to end their existences. Wide Boys were dead boys.

Stupid thing is that Sally-Ann asserts, to this very day, that she was arranging a loan to help Big Herb buy her a ring and a house deposit. And she never married at all, these thirty years later, so smitten was she with that silly oaf, Big Herb.

The Ipswich (Queensland, Australia) Writing Group was given a picture - page 29 - and asked to write a story that came from it. The above was my story.

Getting Knotted

Like a many-fingered fist of knots, our lives seem bound and choked, with little space for us.

Somehow, imperceptibly, the tasks we're given sneak up on us and multiply, like a plague of locusts stripping us bare. These daily tasks grind us into submission on the marble slab, awaiting the slide into a rotting casket.

How we get so tied up in red tape, "to do" lists, oughtism and shoulds is a mystery. It seems that the more we give in to the demands on our time, energy and expertise, the more the demands grow beyond our ability to cope.

You see, we all pretend we're coping but few of us really are. We're all wearing the smiling masks and being ever so nice and looking capable and acting like we've got it together and, and, and …

The biggest mystery, perhaps, is that the things we love doing are the things we put off for later … often never doing them, even by the time we hit the marble slab and rotting casket.

Usually, we start with the most hated jobs demanded of us, just to get them done and out of the way … well, that's what we tell ourselves. The reality is that we think so little of ourselves that we think our own needs and desires are so much less important. In fact, our not doing things for ourselves is the sure sign we think little of ourselves … if we do nothing for ourselves, we think nothing of ourselves.

We can begin to undo this clawing process by prying back the fingers round the knot of our lives – the demands of those who clench us up and squeeze the juice from our drying and withered lives – one by one.

We might phone a mate and say we can't help hang those doors for him.

We might tell our wife we want to take an hour out, by ourselves, for a bike ride or a read at a café.

We might resign from one of the committees we're on … or, at least, take a break from one.

We might tell our boss we can't work past 6.00 pm any more.

In each of these conversations, we don't need to give a reason or an excuse. We can just say it's what we need to do or it doesn't feel right any more.

If we give a reason or excuse, we'll have two problems:

1. It will sound as if we're not sure of our decision, and
2. Every excuse gives the other person an opening to find a way round it and we get roped back into what we didn't want to do.

So, your mission this week is to pry back one of the fingers that are squeezing juice from your life. A short, no-excuses talk and you're a little more free.

And next week? Well, of course that's up to you – do you want to get knotted or not?

The Soft Man

There was a soft man in a hard country - a country of sand, searing heat and tough people. This soft man was not so tough. He could not work as hard as the other sweating farmers, strong millers or wily thieves. He could not be a policeman as he was not as tough on the thieves as he should be. He could not work in the banks or in law firms as he did not like being tough on his customers.

He tried or considered each of the forty-seven prescribed occupations for men in this tough land and found that he could not fit into any of them. So he became a man without an occupation and that meant being a man without support. He had no way to earn the money to acquire the house, the car, the swimming pool, the wife or the other Things that made a man feel important - the Things that everybody always got but envied before they were got. This envy of those who had, created status and made the havers feel important.

This soft man could feel no envy as he really did not want any of those Things. The Things he yearned for (and he yearned for them with a vengeance) were Things on the Inside - love, peace, self-esteem, happiness, nature, friends and a daily chat with his God. It seemed to him that these Inside Things still took a lot of effort to obtain but, once obtained, they could never be taken away or ruined by others. You didn't have burglars or enemies stealing or damaging these sort of Things. You didn't need insurance or security alarm to protect your security. And your security was extremely portable.

There was just one draw-back though - you couldn't use your security as an excuse to get out of things you disliked:

"I cannot go to the football, Joe, as I have to paint the house." Or

"I can't take you children to the park this afternoon because I have to clean the pool" or the car or fix the toilet or the gate or whatever else comes to mind.

If your security is only Inside Things then you have no excuses and you are forced to be honest. You have to say things like:

"I won't go to the football, Joe, as I do not like watching it." Or

"I will not take you children to the park this afternoon as I need a little time to myself."

And far from being upset, Joe or the children or whoever, didn't feel upset as they liked honesty more than they liked football or the park or whatever. They always knew if someone was lying to them or not. They knew that the soft man was always honest and they loved him for it.

It was quite hard for him to be honest at first but, as he practised, he became better. He had more practice than others as he had no excuses. The better at honesty he became, the more loved he became and that made him feel better because love was one of the Things he yearned for with a vengeance. And that love meant friends and he yearned for them, too, with a vengeance.

The other reason he became terribly honest was that he had no occupation. He had never been trained how to think and, therefore, had to work things out for himself. If he didn't know the answer to something he would look people in the eye and say:

"I don't know, but I will find out." Because he didn't know much he ended up finding out a lot. Because he found out a lot, people would ask him many things and he would look them in the eye and say:

"I don't know, but I will find out." And the more he said he didn't know (about every subject imaginable) the more people respected his great knowledge.

Learning many things (including things about himself) gave him self-esteem and being able to pass on that knowledge to others made him happy. Self-esteem and happiness were two Things he yearned for with a vengeance.

Because he had no occupation he was able to spend much time with nature - under trees, with animals and birds, by rivers, in the rain - and it was very peaceful.

Without even planning for it, the Things he had wanted with a vengeance started turning up. Sometimes he didn't realise he had the Things he wanted until some time after he had had them. It was nice though.

The other funny thing was that the Outside Things also started turning up. Because he was honest, shopkeepers would ask him to mind their shops and would then give him food clothes and other Things as a "thankyou". Because of his search for knowledge, many people would come to him for advice or training on things - especially Inside Things. There were so few teachers of the Inside Things and everybody needs to know about their Insides. And so he would get money and other Things for doing that and other things.

Many people would tell him of their personal problems because he was so honest that he would never tell anyone else about it. As a good listener he would help them solve their own problems. For that, too, many would thank him with Outside Things and he became quite wealthy.

So, what is the moral of this little story? The soft man doesn't really know for he doesn't know what it is like to have your mind changed, by someone else, for an occupation. Also, he doesn't know what it is like to want what other people have. What he has, cannot be taken from him and his mind is at rest.

And he wishes the same for you.

Divorcing Our Parents

Robert Bly, the American writer and poet with an immense presence in the Men's Movement, tells us there is a formula for raising boys to men: At birth the boy must marry his mother. Then, some time in early teens, he must divorce his mother and marry his father. Then, when he's about to leave home, he must divorce his father and marry a female man.

What this means, in less poetic language, is that the first years of a boy's life are centred round his mother, attached to her nipple and then around the home, learning about the world of the home-maker.

Then, as his horizons expand, he needs a father to take him out into the exterior world to learn that which his father can teach him – work and outer activities.

Later, he must leave the nest and the healthy boy, having learned the practical and emotional lessons from his parents, must find his way by himself. At this time, he is well served by finding a stern and caring mentor to fall back on.

This is the ideal, according to Robert Bly and most indigenous cultures follow this rule.

For example, the aborigine boys stay with the women for their first years, caring for the home and playing with toys. They're given the boomerang and taught to throw this toy that is never used for hunting. Then, at around twelve to fifteen years, they're taken aside by the men and taught the men's business – hunting and caring for the tribe. At this stage, the toy boomerang is replaced by the kali, the heavy non-returning boomerang; the weapon for killing, along with the spear and club. Then, around six years later, the kadaiche men sneak into the men's space in the dead of night and steal the young men. There are mock battles in which the elders fight with the fathers and, always, the boys are dragged off by the triumphant kadaiche men. This battle adds a drama and a finality to their time with the fathers – yet another cord-cutting ritual. The boys are then taught the spiritual nature of their existence and then sent out to the desert for a year, having been well schooled in how to survive such an ordeal, both physically and mentally.

Their return to the tribe is celebrated by all in a massive corroboree, telling the boys they are now well and truly men and must carry that honour and burden from now on.

This practice of handing the boys from mothers to fathers to mentors is carried out in an almost identical way in most indigenous cultures. The author experienced part of the elders' treatment of young men when taken from their fathers – in South Africa he was taken by the Sangorna, the witch doctors, and told to squat on a bench above the dirt floor of a tiny shed for three days. The shed door was locked. For those silent, hot, dark and mind-screaming days, he could hear the six king cobras slithering round six inches below him, knowing that a sound or movement would alert them to his presence. All he had was his discipline of mind to stay calm and empty, a procedure he had been taught during the preceding weeks. Terrifying though the three days were, the experience taught him more about himself than three years at any university could ever do.

Such rituals and practices are rarely available in the western world where so many boys are brought up by single mothers and taught by female teachers; where fathers perform clerical, non-tactile work that has no interest for young, virile men; where work places are not open to visitors of the younger kind; where so many men hate their work and wish none of it on their sons; where health and safety rules forbid young people from experiencing the reality and risks their parents endure; where the only mentors they have are dysfunctional heroes on television and computer screens.

Robert Bly's contention is that over 80% of television sitcoms portray the man as the village idiot because the producers, writers and directors have yet to divorce their mothers; having not experienced healthy relationships with the fathers and their father's world, they see men through a jaundiced and scathing perception.

The indigenous peoples' treatment of young men can appear as barbaric and "uncivilised" but it generally results in less crime and antisocial behaviour and more balanced and caring men. It's not perfect, of course, and the cynic can always point to a measure of dysfunction … but so can anyone to any society.

What is clear is that the "civilised" way of raising men is not working. The highest number of suicides are from men in the eighteen to twenty five age bracket. Roughly one in every thirty two Americans are under some sort of criminal justice system control and, in Australia, males account for 82% of prison inmates. Rape and abuse crimes – mainly by males – continue to rise. Any number of statistics can be found for the malfunctioning males in our modern world and they are accompanied by the statistics showing the growing pampering and dumbing down of young men's natural instincts to explore their world, to court and experience danger and pain and to learn that caring for their family and community requires discipline more than a pretty smile.

We are struggling to find answers to these rising problems and most "answers" come in the form of more control in every area of our lives – swimming pool fences, seat-belts, bike helmets, health and safety rules … the rules go on. I can't speak for girls – I aren't one – but I suspect they, too, need to experience their world with more freedom and more guidance … guidance being the opposite of control.

Many men's groups throughout the world have set up mentoring initiatives, especially in poorer areas of western society. These quiet movements are making a massive difference to the young men who are looking for someone to fall back on – a female man, if you like – when life becomes too difficult and when the answers out there are only about constriction and not about healthy expansion.

Our current way is not working so it's time to explore other ways … maybe we should ask the young people! Oops, sorry, silly idea … what would they know?

Girls Can Do Anything ... Almost

When a man and a woman come together in wholeness, it is the most beautiful and rare cf things. When each person is whole within themselves - contented, fulfilled, self-realised and need-less (though not desire-less) - and there is complete love and acceptance for the other, as they are, the world sees the glow and is more joyful.

However, very few of us have that wholeness - most of us have some emotional wound(s) or scar(s), yet to be healed. And, as like attracts like, so we attract partners with similar wounds. Caroline Myss calls this "woundology" and if, say, a woman has not been able to resolve (within) the abuse she had from her father, she will most likely attract an abusive partner. And if a man has been "trained" to hide his feelings ("Big boys don't cry") he could easily attract a partner who will not allow him to express himself. Or, the same man may attract a partner who needs and demands of him that he express his feelings, thereby ripping the plaster from an unhealed wound, a wound he is ashamed of but knows not how to heal. And we know not the pain we cause when we're being helpful, sometimes, especially when the other person cannot talk of that pain.

No one can heal the pain of another and no one has the responsibility for another's pain. We can be there, we can support, we can listen but we cannot resolve - that has to come from the bearer of the pain. And, until that pain is healed, situations and people will come in to remind, to exacerbate, to expose, to challenge, to annoy - until something is done by the bearer to attempt a healing. When the honest intention of self-healing is there, then the universe sends in the listeners, the friends, the allowers. But not until the intention is there.

It is very natural for a person to look to others for help. And our motherly and fatherly instincts naturally incline us to want to help, to salve another's wounds. But if the bearer of the pain expects the healing to come from outside of hirself , it will remain and gnaw forever.

And so, it is easy for opposite sexes to shame each other, to expose the wounds of the other, for that is what is meant to be. If a mother has shamed her son by demanding that he express his emotions, he will close down more and will invariably attract a partner who demands the same, until he heals his own "mother wound". Although his partner is giving him a gift (to see what healing he needs to do) he may, instead, retaliate and expose a wound of his partner with sulking or abuse. This is woundology. It is not important who starts the cycle - that the cycle continues and accelerates is the true sadness.

The universe often provides a partner or other woman (friend, counselor, etc.) to point out the man's wound, but it can seldom be healed in the presence of a woman. One woman cannot repair the damage done by another. For most men, powerlessness usually envelops him when trying to deal with emotions in front of a woman, for he knows how clever she is at expression while he is a complete dumbo. A person hears what they hear and if a man has had 30 or so years of hearing (from mothers, teachers, writers, television, partners) he is not good at expression; that is what he knows of himself. He is good with a hammer, but when it comes to emotional stuff, that's what women are good at. He's not.

It is a biological fact that women are better at combining feelings with expression - they often master it at 14, while many men are still struggling with it past 40 years. Add to that biological difference with a mixture of "boys don't cry" stuff, along with a constant feeling of being inadequate and the whole realm of feelings becomes so overwhelming the man doesn't know where to start. Easier to leave well alone. Many women complain that their men do not show their feelings but the sad fact is that, for many men, when they look down (inside) there is nothing there. They are hiding nothing for there is nothing to hide. They simply do not know what their feelings are for they have been buried so deep, they are unreachable. So deep they don't know they're there.

Therefore, for many men, the only safe way to start this process is with other men - with others who will not bring up the risk of shaming, who will not finish their sentences, who will not bring back all those past inadequacies. It doesn't matter how understanding and patient a woman is, she still has a woman's body and, especially for vulnerable men, that is a formidable reminder of pains from other women. It doesn't matter how understanding and loving I am, I (as a man) am probably not going to be much comfort to a girl who has just been raped. I have a man's body and that reminds her too much of her pain from a man.

It is very difficult today, for there are many women without partners, bringing up boys. These women do their best. They really try hard, but there are some things a mother (or any other woman) cannot give her young man. Robert Moore (from Chicago) says to men: "Have you admired a younger man in the past week? Have you been admired by an older man in the past week? If you are a young man and you are not being admired by an older man, you are being hurt." Strong words.

Robert Bly talks of the five-stage process of becoming a man - bonding with your mother, separation from your mother, bonding with your father, separation from your father, the appearance of the "male mother" or mentor. We do not do the separation from our mothers very well and nor do we bond with our fathers well. Often there is no father to bond with - he is either separated from our mother or he is always away (physically and mentally) for his work. Often the short-cut is taken, which is to shame our father and this is seen in the numerous sitcoms on television where the man is the idiot, while the woman is sensitive and intelligent - the writers are trying to short-cut their growth to manhood, as are those enjoying the shaming of men.

So what are the mothers to do? As hard as they try, they can only give the boys mothering and perhaps look for a male to admire and take some interest in the young man - a mentor. This mentor does not have to have a daily or weekly commitment to the boy, but someone the boy knows holds him in his heart is vital. Beyond that, monthly contact may be all that's needed. This mentor is not so easy to find as most grandfathers live somewhere else. Most boys do not have this "male mother" around, someone who is interested in their soul, a man to hold them in their heart, to listen and to guide. The result is so often that the boys carry out their own initiation by driving fast cars, stealing and damaging property. They get the attention of the police and this attention of these older men is better than nothing. This male attention is something a mother cannot give, something a girlfriend or wife cannot give.

That there are so many older men sitting in rest-homes and retirement villages, feeling redundant and worthless, is a great shame. Their wisdom, experience, patience, non-attachment and so many other things are part of the soul of our community that is being wasted. We talk a lot about our youth being our future, but without the wisdom of the elders, I wonder what our future will be. The older men have the time to give and the youth are seeking it (in their unique way) and I wonder why we cannot get them together.

All my life I have looked and asked for an older man to be there to talk to, to listen to, to be with and to absorb from. I still look for that old man. I have heard sixty year old men say they would still like an older man to hold them in their heart, as they would like to do for men younger than them. So, old man, you are important and wanted and a young man is any man younger than you. I use the word "old" without shame for you have so much to give.

I, therefore, put out a call: If there are any older men who would like to be there for the younger ones, please step forward and let me know. Also, if there are any younger men (or mothers) looking for a mentor, also come forward and write. Let's see the circle of life complete itself and us all become more whole.

Trial And Nearer

We bought our first house in 1973 for $17,750 and we borrowed something like $17,000. It had been built in 1902 and had had little improvements since then. The floor was shaky and uneven, the roof rusting, the paint and wallpaper were peeling inside and out and it was full of a very busy family of borers who had flicked their dust everywhere. Years later Mum admitted that when she first saw the house, she went home and cried all night, feeling sorry for her son living in such a run-down hovel. But we saw nothing but potential – move this wall to there, put in windows here, change this, add that and pretty soon we'd have a charming cottage, with our own imprint, to live in for a very long time.

Apart from three weeks working for Brian Cunliffe, a builder, some four years earlier, I had no building experience. My father, the perfectionist, could not abide anything done by anyone unless they were an expert with at least 250 years' experience.

I had once collected what scraps of wood I could find – mostly flimsy apple-box wood – and made myself a sledge to scream down grassy hills. The wood was crap and my seven-year-old carpentry skills were crap but I was inordinately proud of my new creation which had taken hours to cobble together and days to plan. I had a sneaking suspicion that it might not last a life-time or my bodily weight and I looked forward to the process of trying it out and continually improving it.

My father saw it quite differently. Snatching it from my gently cradling arms, he tossed it into a broken heap, explaining, "Good God, man, that's a complete mess! It's already fallen apart so I'll show you a sledge." He shoved me aside and, after two days, appeared with THE PERFECT sledge. It was beautifully sculpted – nailed, screwed and glued, sanded to polished perfection – it was heavy enough to have sunk the Titanic faster than an iceberg and accounted for the massive shoulders I soon developed. I used it a few times and it went downhill splendidly owing to its weight and waxing, to the deep consternation of two sheep and a dog – their mothers now miss them deeply. However, getting the beast uphill proved too arduous and I'm sure future archaeologists will gaze in wonder at it as they ponder the possibility that gravity was more of a challenge in this era than theirs.

In that and so many other ways, I found myself unable to experiment with construction and, quite suddenly, 20 years later, I had a whole house to experiment with.

I went to the local council to apply for a permit to renovate the house. I'd sketched some rough ideas on a scrap of paper and explained what we might do with the house. For $10 the building inspector gave us a permit that said, "Alterations as per owners' needs." In other words, we could do anything we liked and we never saw a building inspector. No one checked on us at all.

Some say it's good we didn't know what we didn't know but I would do it all again in a trice. In fact we did it three more times and I love taking a building mess and turning it into something creatively liveable. I also love doing things people say I can't. The kitchen ceiling was tongue-and-groove (i.e. large grooves along it) and many, many layers of paint had been slavered over the pitted and gouged surface. It was beyond redemption and had to be covered up somehow – heavily embossed wallpaper seemed the best idea we had for it.

The man at the decorator shop said no one could wallpaper a ceiling. I told him it was gloss paint and, with an astonished and then dismissive look said, "You definitely can't do that. Don't bother." I then said I was going to use heavily embossed paper and he took on a scared-rabbit look and I feared he was about to walk out on his job as he patiently (as to a stupid child) explained, "You definitely, definitely, definitely can't do that. Sell the house NOW!" I insisted he sell me the embossed paper, paid quickly and then made a dash for it before he had time to alert the local mental home of my whereabouts, to take me away. I sanded the worst of the eruptions and craters, made up my own secret sizing recipe, made up my own secret glue recipe and, together,

Sandy and I papered and painted the ceiling. It looked stunning … so stunning, in fact, that the real estate agent (quite unbeknown to us till much later) told prospective buyers that the house had a pressed-zinc ceiling.

I taught myself carpentry, plumbing, electrical wiring, roofing, wallpapering, painting, brickwork, concreting, glazing and a few other skills and it became my obsession.

After seven years we doubled our money on that house, doubled it again in four years in Taupo and did the same in Rotorua and Tauranga.

I also reveled in the realization that I had skills I'd previously had no knowledge of. I just had to start a job and my body and mind would make it happen. It was an adventure and everything was possible. Sadly, I see mothers telling little Timmy not to climb a tree as he might fall and hurt himself and so many people trying to protect us from ourselves. I see so many people holding themselves back from attempting the possible for some unknown (and unlikely, usually) creature from the dark which will arise and devour them. We're forced to wear bicycle helmets, seat belts and fence our pools for fear of injury. But I learned to drive the Land Rover at twelve years old and had to drive it over treacherous country roads and we all just did that. We rode dangerous horses and swam in unfenced rivers and, yes, we got hurt. But we got up again with the realization of a new limitation and determination for ourselves.

And then people wonder and shake their heads at the young people (mainly men) who drive their cars at mad speeds and take all sorts of risks – they're going to test themselves out some way or another and if that is stifled early on, they'll just do it later. What most people don't realize is that that later we leave it to allow them to do their boundary-testing, the more frustration and pent-up anger goes into it … and the more dangerous it is for others. Better to allow it in their toddler years than stifle it till their late teens or much later to come out as political leaders who love to damage whole populations and environments.

Protective devices do not stop people damaging themselves – they only stop us thinking adventurously. They implant a timidity, an obedience that stops us questioning any insane authority and any insane rule they put upon us … for our own good!

My father had kept me "safe" from making imperfect sledges and huts in the trees but, eventually, I had to break out into self-discovery and find that, by creating imperfection over and over, I could eventually teach myself to create beauty.

Many of the Beatles' first songs were crap and many of Picasso's paintings were crap. But they kept creating and creating and creating and then beautiful music and art arose.

If we stop people before they make their first, imperfect move, the world is denied great beauty.

I Am A Candle

Some see the injustice in this world,
And are driven to stamp it out.
Our politicians, our missionaries and our radicals,
See only one perfection - their own.

They take the world, its people, like a potter,
And force a shape of their own ideal,
Never once asking the clay,
If it liked being the way it was.

Some see the injustice in this world,
And knowing it is not for them,
Our hermits, our loners and our apathetic,
Seek out a sanctuary, a haven apart.

They don't interfere, just leaving well alone,
In their sanctuary of the hills and nature,
Or a haven in the mind - space tripping and dreaming.
"Leave me alone, and I'll return when you're better."

Some see the injustice in this world,
And want to express it with beauty.
Our artists, our writers and our musicians,
Giving grace to ugliness and change.

They put forth their view as an image,
Of sorrow and joy, of dreams and hopes.
Their inspiration may become ours, if we choose.
They bare their soul, but not their fangs.

I see the world as it is and love it.
I see the world as I would like it, and love it more.
I stand tall and straight, true to myself.
My flame, my vision, for me - not for setting others alight.

If you come to my light we are both blessed.
If you choose another candle I wish you well.
A candle doesn't sulk, it just is ... and "just is" is justice.

Shopping for Peace

He has the personality of a shopping trolley. You know, the one with the dodgy wheel that you constantly swear at. Whatever way you push, cajole or encourage, he'll always go the other way; the other way that's right back at you! So you leave him there, objecting about everything and everyone, wondering why everything and everyone leaves him there.

It's a lonely life being irascible and none of us know the benefits. He's angry and alone while we toddle off in our peaceful, puzzled way. Yes, we're drawn back, one by one, one at a time, to see how he is, see if he's changed. The magnet is guilt; guilt at seeing him suffer, guilt at seeing him angry, guilt at seeing him alone.

Perhaps it's the need to feel needed, wanted and useful. Perhaps it's the need to feel like we're in control; if we show enough concern and wisdom he just might listen and mellow out. We know he won't but we keep trying, vainly hoping he'll see some light in his darkness, some shred of humour in his grimness. But he doesn't and he never will.

Though I hate to admit it, I must concede that he and I are alike in more ways than I feel comfortable with. You see, we're both irrevocably determined. Stubborn, even. We want things our way. The only way.

For some unnatural reason, we just can't let things go, can't let them be. Immovable Reality is there for us to push against, argue about, battle with.

It's personal. It always has been. It always will be.

The whole stupid, irrational system was set up to annoy us, get under our skin. Others aren't bothered by the things that bother us.

They don't care. We do.

It's personal.

The difference is he's fighting to annoy people and I'm fighting to please people. Damned if I know but no one's any happier or less annoyed or better off ... or any grumpier, more annoyed or worse off. No one cares.

Yeah, I know. All my arguing and battling get me nowhere, nohow, never. But, damn it, why can't he just be a little agreeable ... you know, let his guard down, admit I'm right, just once in a while.

They say sons take after their fathers but that's not right. Not with us. I try so hard to have him happy and he tries so hard to make everyone annoyed.

So, we're opposites ... right?

The Good Book

For sixteen clashing years they've been trying to shape me like a big cheese they let stand to get stinky. But I don't fit. I pretend to but I don't.

My body's here but my mind's other places, like, I do the milking regularly, before and after school, but I'm winter, thinking I'm spring and yearning for summer. Unexpected ideas pour in unexpectedly and mercilessly.

My wife's arranged, years ago, and I should be grateful; she's a nice, reliable girl, Mary is. But I thought there was, love – you know, heart-pounding, sweaty-hand stuff – and I've never felt that. Folks here don't show it so maybe I'm making it up. How would I know?

I'm told to be content but, content? Content's okay but I'd love some happy, silly and amazing too. Not all the time as it might get tiring. Once in a while it'd be nice.

Anyway, these city people came to our community and everybody said they looked weird and different though we shouldn't judge, be kindly forgiving and spiritual. Anyway, I judged them – I judged on the good side but still judged – and the only word that fitted was sharp. They wore these suits and I felt so slovenly next to them. I really, really wanted to talk to them and find out about where they came from. Must be a different world; a smooth suits, shiny shoes, clean fingernails and brushed hair world.

Ma said they're inspecting papers, whatever that means, and everyone's treating them with the reverence they have for the Good Book. But I told myself they're just humans underneath and I might never see them again, my chance gone. I had to do something – bump into them, start a conversation, anything. I prayed on it but Da kept me so busy outside I couldn't get near.

Then I had an idea. They're inspecting papers so they like what's written on them. I snuck into the shed cupboard and got Da's notepad for recording sick cows. I prayed for God to send me some nice and impressive words. None came and I nearly swore. I tried not to get angry but couldn't stop it. Here was my chance and I was letting it slip under the gate.

I hate to say it because it's unholy … respect your parents and all … but I couldn't stop thinking I really wanted to leave his place. I'd thought this before, many times, but I'd always been able to bless and release the thoughts. Not this time – it just wouldn't go.

I ripped out some pages and stuffed them and the pencil in my pocket, hoping God would find time, soon, to send me words for my deliverance. And hoped Da wouldn't find them gone else I'd be sent to the Repentance Room and have to confess and all that tedious and embarrassing stuff.

Patience was a virtue, they said. I finished the milking, fed the calves and cleaned up and it was dinner time. The sun had gone and I knew they'd gone too. Unholy words came to my throat but I didn't utter them. Nearly did but I didn't. I sat on a trough and tried really hard not to cry or blaspheme and kept it all in.

"That was big sigh, young man."

"What!" I asked, leaping up in shock. There was one of the sharp people there; a lady in smooth black and white.

"I'm sorry, I startled you," she said with the kindest smile, putting her little phone in her pocket. "Why are you looking so pensive?" She sat down and patted the space next to her. I sat too.

Pensive? I'd never heard that word and it sounded nice. Expensive and nice.

"I'm … well, I'm trying to think of something to write to you," I said. Last chance. No use being dumb and stupid. Speak up honestly, though I'm feeling hot, red and shaking.

"Do you write?"

"Mmm, yeah, I do. Stories that come into my brain," I said. I'd never told anyone before as it wasn't exactly the words of the Good Book. "Please don't tell Ma and Da." Somehow, she looked really trusty.

"I'd love to see them." She smiled and lit the sky up; pale sweet light.

"Would you? Gosh," I said. No one had seen my secret words and God sent her to me like I asked. "It's in my room and no girls are allowed."

"Can you bring them out?"

"If I go in I'll have to wash and have dinner and you'll be gone."

"We're back tomorrow so drop them out your window, now, and we'll talk about it then, after I've read them."

We did that and they weren't there the next day. They'd gone. I felt a hollow in my stomach, like a mealy worm was crawling round, chewing my insides. I hid behind the shed and couldn't stop the tears and cursing this time and I didn't care who heard me.

I heard a laugh behind me and spun around to see her silhouette glowing in the sunset.

"Sorry, Samuel, I didn't mean to laugh … I just, aah, haven't heard you cry or anything," Mary said, her small voice trailing off.

"Well I do," I huffed, not caring what she thought.

"You're always, mmm, constrained, like everyone here," she said, coming closer. "I thought only I had feelings."

"You never look like you have any."

"I've got more than my body can hold. I have to let them out when no one's looking," she said, her voice growing bolder. "I thought I was weird."

I stood up and could feel her breath on my face. I itched to touch her but that was forbidden. This wasn't the Mary I had known all my life; this one had a spark and I started feeling my heart-pounding, my hands sweaty.

"Oh Mary," I said and touched her cool shoulder. She didn't pull away and I sensed her smile as the dusk gathered its dark cloak. I longed to tell her of my writing and my lost opportunity but words wouldn't come.

"Shall we meet here tomorrow?" she asked.

"Yes," I said and she fled.

We started meeting in our secret place most evenings and I eventually told her of my writing. I feared she'd report me but I had to tell someone as the story was bursting to get out. She listened, smiled and patted my arm and the tingles from that went through my whole body for days afterwards.

Maybe six months later, a parcel came and I had to open it in front of my family. No secrets, see. It was a package of six identical books. They had a black and white picture of a boy sitting on a trough, like he was thinking, and were called The Dairy Diaries. I trembled to open the first book but couldn't stop while my Ma and Da and brothers stared silently, unmoving. Yes, here were my stories, all nicely typed up. Someone had copied them and made a book. I shut the book and stared at the cover again and saw my name, Samuel Brightwell, at the bottom.

I felt that heart-pounding, sweaty-hand stuff that I had with Mary, oftimes.

I handed a book to Da but his hands didn't move and nor did his face. He was frozen. I handed it to Ma and she didn't move. Her eyes were as soft and wet. Da's were hard and dry.

"You bin keeping secrets, lad?" Da asked, his voice quiet and rough.

"I ... I didn't know books were being made, Da. I promise."

"You bin writing words of yer own? Not of the Good Book?" he asked, his hands clenching and unclenching.

"Yes," I mumbled.

"They's of the devil and I'll no touch them. Burn them!" he ordered.

"But Seth ..." Ma said as tears flowed more freely.

"Now!" he commanded.

"No," I said quietly. Firmly. I don't know where the firmly came from but it just seemed to rise from the earth and I couldn't stop it. This was something that was mine, something I was proud of, though it mystified me ... how the books came to be made. But they were mine and they were good. Good books. I knew that.

Da stepped forward and I stepped back with the ripped-open parcel in my arms. I bumped into Ma and she touched my shoulder.

"Can we think on this, Seth? Pray on it, perhaps," she suggested.

"Out now and burn them. You're blaspheming God and our household," he said, his voice rising. "We canna' have this."

"I'll take the books, Ma, and go," I said, trying to smile at her. I looked at my younger brothers and they looked away.

"Please Samuel ..." she implored, her fingers digging into my shoulder. She somehow knew I might not be back. I hugged her and my books all together and then rushed out the door. Mary was waiting. It was too dark to see them properly but I handed her one and she held it like it was a fragile baby. She seemed to know it was special.

"It's my words. My writing, Mary," I said. "I don't know how it happened and Da says I must burn them." I sniffed and wiped my eyes.

"Come here you big lump." She wrapped her arms around me –first time ever – and I didn't ever want to leave that circle of sweetness. My eyes burst like fountains and my body shook as a huge cry came up my body. She held me like she'd never let me go and I howled in her ear and dribbled down her neck and I think she was smiling. She may have been crying too. Not sure.

"We have three choices," she said when I was quieter, holding me at arm's length. "Pretend you've burned them."

"I can't lie."

"Burn them and pretend they never happened."

"Can't do that. Can't burn what comes from my heart. Just can't."

"Or leave this place with your books."

"And leave you?" Leaving my family seemed easier than leaving Mary, just then. Actually, I just couldn't.

"I'm where you are, Samuel. I'll come if you want me to," she said simply, unemotionally, as if it was just a fact.

I slumped down on the trough and probably looked like the boy on the cover ... hey, maybe it was me, I suddenly thought. Mary sat next to me, her arm round my shoulder as a hundred thoughts tumbled round in my brain. I couldn't stop one of them and looked at Mary with a dumb smile.

"This a defining moment," she said.

"You'll take the fourth choice." We both leapt up at Ma's voice in the dark. "You'll stay with your aunt Maud, my sister who left our community all those years ago. I've packed your bag."

"But Ma ..." I said as a squillion questions tumbled into my mouth. "You knew?"

"I knew all along, son. You've always had the writing gift but not the gift of secrecy. You weren't always careful of putting your words away and I read them and loved them and waited for the time you would stand for your passion."

"Da will be angry. He'll stop us."

"The fearsome are so as they're fearful," she said, touching my arm.

"Fear thinks crooked. Love is strength and love thinks straight; it needs not to change. He'll change his mind when his fear goes."

"But Mary?" I asked as another question unravelled itself.

"She can visit, for now, and we'll let time and love take care of the future."

"The books? The suit people?"

"Aye, I had a wee chat with her," she said, coming closer. "Seems her brother is a publisher. Some secrets are good, Samuel. I wanted to see the look on your face." She grabbed Mary and I and we hugged and chuckled and cried a little in the dark.

This was written for the Newcastle, Australia short story competition - it didn't win!

Ordinary Adventures

I met a man who ran a factory, a factory that made furniture - things for sitting upon. He was an ordinary bloke who smoked and joked and talked in a foreign accent. His factory (he didn't actually own it as he was an ordinary bloke) was quite ordinary too and the sit-upon things it made were nice and comfortable but did nothing especially memorable - it just supported a lot of bums.

I gradually got to know him over a few months and it soon became apparent that 'ordinary' wasn't a very good word for him. I'm not sure what it was but ordinary wasn't. You see, behind his ordinary "factory manager" label, his ordinary factory, ordinary clothes and other ordinary bits, he was a bit of an adventurer. He didn't actually climb the Matterhorn on his hands; hop across the Arctic on one leg, naked; swim the Adriatic with both legs tied to a brick or undertake any other body-risking venture. He wasn't that sort of adventurer, but in his ordinary every-day life he had an adventure every day. These weren't Earth-shattering, front-page-news types of adventures that you would write about (though I am) but they were very real adventures for him. And, without them, his life-force would certainly have withered and died.

He started working life in his family's furniture business and that was an adventure because, before then, he hadn't done that. He learned to cut and sew and upholster and each new learning was a thing to be cherished and improved upon. And each new design and fabric was savoured and remembered. He designed, bought materials, built and then went out and sold his creations. Each sale was an adventure, as were the friendships and ideas he got from his customers. Nothing was boring and even the complaints and rejects were fun for they took him on a new adventure of doing things better.

Then he moved house, from England to New Zealand, and that was an adventure - kinda' scary and kinda' fun. He ran furniture stores, managed furniture factories and immersed himself in every aspect of his trade. Some thought he was a little unstable, having so many jobs, but he was happy finding and meeting every new challenge. He was recently asked to design 15 new lounge suites and so he designed 25 - he just couldn't help himself. Each day he drives 2 hours to and from work and many people might find that boring, but not him. Every day is different - different weather, different routes, different traffic jams - and all the while his mind is surfing over new waves of ideas.

For 30 years he has been in the same business and some may find that boring, but not him. There is always a different pleat, a different chair-arm shape, a different customer, a different sunset. He knows he doesn't have to go to Spain to run with the bulls, to the Sahara to smell the desert, to India to meet a guru; to have an adventure. He can wake up, open his eyes and say "Wow, they do open", and that's an adventure. He turns on the shower and exclaims, "Wow, hot water still comes out," with glee.

Of course, being an ordinary bloke, he does get depressed, angry, sad and all those other things us ordinary folks get. But somehow, his anger, sadness, depression or whatever, lasts for only a flicker (compared to yours and mine) for it isn't long before another adventure, another challenge, turns up - his eyes sparkle, he grins and surfs another wee wave.

The other day he had a car accident - his car couldn't be driven but he was O.K., apart from a few bruises. He could have sat and stared at the car, moaning about other drivers, the cost of repair and a hundred other things but, no, he rang a friend and while he waited, he got out his sketch pad and had fun designing new couches. It sounds quite a practical attitude and reminds me of something I heard yesterday on the radio:

"There are only 2 things to worry about:
Whether you are well or sick.
If you are well you have nothing to worry about.

If you are sick you only have 2 things to worry about:
Whether you will get better or not.
If you will get better you have nothing to worry about.
If you are going to die you only have 2 things to worry about:
Whether you are going to heaven or to hell.
If you are going to heaven you have nothing to worry about.
And if you are going to hell you are going to be so busy shaking hands with old friends you won't have any time to worry."

This guy will probably never be a film-star or great politician or sporting hero, but his quiet love and acceptance of life inspires more than any of the grandest achievers or speakers - perhaps it's because his attitude is (like me) very simple or perhaps it is because he is simply doing it, not just talking about it.

The trouble is, being an ordinary bloke, I am finding it hard to actually live it, though I try, and I worry about that …

For Crying Out Loud

It's funny how our greatest achievements are often the ones we get no medals for. Sometimes we don't know of, or acknowledge, those achievements until long afterwards.

I have only learned to cry in the last five years. My need and my compassionate friends have been the greatest catalyst for the change. A spell in a men's anger management group also helped and so did life. Sometimes it got so hard that something just had to give. With everything building up inside I felt that I would just explode if I didn't release it in some way or another and anger and blaming just exacerbated the problem. I had to cry and when I did the painful release was so cleansing and freeing, I wondered why I didn't do it long ago.

I have now got to the stage of being able to cry in front of female friends and although I tell myself I can do it with male friends, I have yet to realize that pinnacle of success.

There is still a little way to go, though, as I realized today. I dashed through the rain, leapt into my car and immediately burst into tears. I then realized that I had banged my head on the door-way, getting in, and before registering the bump and the pain, the tears started to roll. I then realized I had learned to cry from emotional pain, but never before had I cried from physical pain.

There was a time, of course, that any pain produced tears but that stopped at around four years of age. The pain didn't stop but the crying did - I learned or was trained not to. Other people felt uncomfortable and it was just not done for a boy to cry. So the falls from horses, motor-bikes and trees, broken collar-bone and many other bodily hurts were endured with four-letter expletives, a brave face and a dollop of anger. This way of dealing with pain was then transferred to that of emotional pain and so my reaction to a friend's or partner's pain became not one of compassion but denial. Anger at the apparent cause of the pain and anyone else close was my remedy. It wasn't that I didn't feel my or others' pain, but from the outside it sure looked like that. Others might (and probably did) have seen me as hard and uncaring and I don't blame them.

Similarly, displays of unbridled joy and exhilaration were frowned on and actively discouraged and so extreme emotions at each end of the spectrum were buried and denied expression.

Looking back with this wonderful hindsight I can see that as I learned to bury the pain and its causes, I became immune to my pain and all other emotions. I could feel horrible or unhappy but had no idea what that unhappiness was - was it anger, jealousy, abandonment, feeling belittled or what? I had no idea. Then about four years ago, driving along, I felt the familiar, grey, indefinable cloud of unhappiness descend and, for some unknown reason, I put my hand on my stomach and asked what the unhappiness was. The answer was immediate. I forget the actual cause of it now, but realized, with great joy, that, for the first time, I was able to specifically identify what the pain, the unhappiness, was. I got no medals for that achievement - I didn't need any. The discovery of a really clever and discerning person within was the greatest gift I could have imagined.

At this time I began to feel great joys arising from within, for no apparent reasons - warm fuzzy stuff I'd never felt before.

I am still refining the detection system and it doesn't always work immediately, especially when the pain is too much to accept and deal with at the time. But it's improving and is a whole lot better than before. The next step of actually dealing with the cause of the pain is, also, less than perfect, but that's another story ....

That was written several years ago and, since then, I have succeeded in crying in front of male friends and, though pretty daunting at first, it's now getting a little easier. The above was written for me only, and is one of the ways I use to deal with things - get it out of me and on to paper. Back then I would never have had the courage to show this to anyone else and expose my frailties - it was bad enough telling myself.

However, having been in several groups of men, by men, for men, I have come to realize (with total amazement) that I'm not the only bloke going through these things and with the same weaknesses. I'm actually quite normal! Perfect in my imperfections! Non-copers of the world unite, you have nothing to gain but your wholeness.

So why was I scared to tell anyone about my imperfect self? Partly because, like so many other men I have talked to, I felt that I was the one who should be able to cope, to be strong and to support others when they were weak and/or confused. I once asked my parents why I had had less support from them than my siblings and Mum said, "Because you've always been the one who coped." I then realized what a brilliant actor I had been and how I had pushed others aside with my pretence of "I'm O.K."

So, here I am today - scared, confident, clever, stupid, funny, boring, sexy, shy, capable, confused and just too blooming lazy to hold up the disguises any more. And I can cry with joy at the amazing feelings inside.

Me Mate's Dead

He wasn't the friendliest mate in the land
Growlin' quickly if'n you wasn't his match
A bit territorial, you understand
Bite your bloody head off, you touch his patch

Had his own funny ways, did he
Never really hated no one
Well, not really all that much, you see
Just testing yer resolve, see how close you come

Chorus
It's about tryin, dyin', cryin', sighin'

Well, yeah, no one lives forever
And me mate passed on Tuesday last
Had a funeral, buried him proper like
Made a speech, spat on dirt, hat at half-mast

And over a beer with the blokes
We got mumblin' how our memories do pass
When the bugger's alive he's the worst of folks
When he's dead we get fonder by the glass

Chorus

Yeah, well, me mate's lyin' in a pile
He did look after, protect, his family's kit
And when you get to know him, took a while
He'd come around to smilin' a bit

So, shed a tear now he's run
Not comin' back, missin' him real bad
Won't be chasing sheep or strangers for fun
The best dog a man ever had

Goodbye mate

Chorus

The Shy Boy

Once upon a time there was a shy boy, a very shy boy. He'd learned that to question and disagree meant pain; that people would hurt him with their gnarly hands, vicious words and dismissive looks. His career came not from any deep, long-held desire but because he couldn't think what else to do and because it was presented to him on a shiny silver platter – great salary and prestige thrown in for free.

He later, much later, realized that it was an attempt to impress a father who had no regard for his son and unabashed regard for professional men. Also, much later, he surmised his choice had come from a dread of rejection – accounting was an occupation in which you were either right or wrong, you knew if you were right or wrong and so could correct anything before anyone else saw it. It left no boggy ground for creativity, that shaky and uncertain quicksand which would suck you into its judgmental maw at the slightest of movements.

One might surmise that shyness would be knocked off a boy as he stumbled through a broken world of criticism and blame, as it bumped into the guilt-ridden who rushed to make themselves right and others wrong. But no, it didn't dissolve or grow immune to constant immersion in the song, *How Great Thou Aren't*. In fact, this boy's shyness grew faster than he did and it clung to him tighter and tighter.

There is, though, a season for all things and at around forty, he began to give into a greater force – a clawing, growing desire to know God – not a religious God but a God that reeked of connection, love, support and peace … a God that gave only that which he'd seldom felt.

Shyness is a lonely pit and, to withdraw from a marriage-less-lived is to fall deeper into that pit. But there comes a time that the fear of release grows smaller than the need for release. Strangely, within moments of taking the forbidding step to leave, a step so long contemplated with dread, he found this strange group of people who hadn't existed in this world before ... well, in *his* world before. They had the same God-filled desires and a fascination for how life worked, just as he'd had all his life. Oh my gosh, he could talk about things he was interested in – God, spirituality, personal development – without being battered about, physically or verbally.

"Man, where have all kind and concerned people been while I was hiding in shyness ... oh, hang on, it was me who was hiding, not them!" he exclaimed to himself.

He soon realised how his life had been controlled and limited by shyness and, more importantly, that he could do something about it – he could shed it as a snake sheds its skin.

So he designed a *Get Rid of Shyness* workshop. It involved only him and the idea was to fully immerse himself in shyness-challenging situations – standing in front of groups of people, for hours on end, every day, teaching them some of what he knew.

The next day he walked into the local polytechnic, asked about teaching positions and the receptionist laughed in his face. This poor, shy chap could have retreated there and then but he'd had enough of running and so stood his ground ... long enough for the laughing to die down and for the receptionist to apologise profusely. She wasn't laughing at him but at the timing. Their accounting lecturer had been fired the previous day and they were desperately looking for a replacement. Then in walks our shy man!

A week later he was standing in front of fifteen students, teaching accounting. And, no, the shyness did not leave easily. He spent the next year petrified on a daily basis and, many times, he'd stand outside a lecture room paralysed, unable to step inside. Many a time this terror urged – no, demanded – that he slink out and never return. But he never did.

A year later he was teaching a Business Communication class and realised he was doing it – he was communicating to a group of people and that there had been no terror for over a month. Without noticing it, the grip of shyness had fallen away and he was free.

The lecturing was meant to be a temporary, fear-releasing process but, over twenty years later, he's I'm still doing it, loving it and he's I'm grateful as it's served me well in many ways, including enabling me to travel much of the world … much of the world a shy boy would never see!

We're All Addicts

Scientists tell us that if they place a frog in hot water it will immediately hop out. However, if they place a frog in cold water and heat it up gradually, the frog will stay there till it's boiled to death.

Now, exchange the frog for us and water for our addictions.

If we see a drunk, an obese person or an addicted gambler, we might quickly decide we don't want to be like them.

However, for them, their addiction didn't happen with shocking suddenness. The drunk started as a tea-totaller (in childhood, at least), began drinking socially (non-addictively) and slowly, day by day, the consumption grew. Right now, we might see her addiction clearer than she can for it has snuck up on her like the hot water for the frog. Similarly for the overeater, gambler and every other addict.

The unnerving thing is that none of us is very different from any addict. In fact, we are all addicted to something, no matter how innocuous it seems. Some people can manage theirs, some can hide theirs and some can do neither. It's the last group we notice and judge.

You see, when we talk of addictions, we initially think of addictions to nicotine, alcohol, drugs, food, work and sex. There are many more subtle addictions like those to life dramas, need for control over people and circumstances, anger, depression, television, computer games, playing victim, being late, being funny, being sarcastic, being poor, cooking and gardening.

Cooking? Gardening? These are addictions? Yes, they can be.

Every one of us finds something about our lives stressful. Whenever we relieve a stress, another one creeps up or us. We may get over the stress of our poverty by getting a well-paid job, only to find the job stressful. Then we have two remedies – one works and the other doesn't.

1. We recognise the stress and do what we can to cope with it, or
2. We bury ourselves in our favourite activity.

Avoidance never works for that skulking shadow of stress is always there. Every time it flashes its vicious teeth and claws at our soul with its poisonous talons, we retreat (yet again) onto our favourite activity – e.g. food, cooking or gardening – more and more. Eventually we realise we're so attached to our favourite activity that our spirit is being boiled to death – it destroys our relationships, finances, careers and/or sense of self. The original stress hasn't gone away and now it's attended by its willing and ugly bride, addiction.

We can judge addicts harshly but it's a gossamer curtain's distance from where we could easily be. And how do we know which side of that fine and fragile curtain we're on? Simply by asking two questions:

1. "Am I able to stop doing this right now, for at least a month?"
2. "Does my doing this impinge on my relationships, finances, career and/or sense of self?" In other words, "If I stopped doing this, would anything in my life improve?"

You know the answer to these questions and honestly admitting the answer to your greatest critic – you – is the best first step you can take.

The next step, of course, is to become really courageous and ask someone else for help. Do not be surprised that, when you finally say, "I've had enough of this addiction. I need help!", help will turn up in your life in the shape of a friend, an overheard conversation, a chance meeting or an honest inquiry.

Perhaps you could try it now. You've nothing to lose as a beautiful surprise, a helping hand, could be waiting for your call.

In And Out We Go

Outward and inward and outward, like our breathing. It's a strange and crooked journey we take, some of us - to the same place we're all going. Rex McCann calls it going home and I can't think of a better phrase. George (I'll call him), alluding to his homosexuality, his life path and the talking stick he was holding, said, "I'm like this stick; there's nothing about me that's straight!" We laughed along with this wise and perceptive man and, in that moment, felt a little closer in our brotherhood as we realized we were all on a winding path to the same place - from our different places of culture, experience, age, sexual preference and perception.

Not too many years ago, what I owned was what I was. I didn't know it at the time, but I valued myself by my professional label, the two cars, the house, the yacht and all the other trappings we had. Many of my acquaintances were similar and, as an accountant, I was welcomed into the Jaycees while my truck-driving friend was given the distinct feeling of being an outsider.

That incident may have started something but the four redundancies, two divorces and business failure certainly ended the outward journey, for where there were no assets there was no me. The inward journey began when I was nothing, had nothing, in a world of ownership. I needed to fill that huge and empty hole within me with something. I tried travel and that led me to the Arunda people in the centre of Australia - people who had nothing but a deep knowing of who they were. A whole and hole-less people.

Relationships provided me with wonderful experiences, pain, joy and good friends. But, in the end, no-one could fill my gaping hole. Sometimes the hole was larger, with less of me.

Frantic activity was great but didn't fill the gap and, though it wasn't for me, I know many who tried alcohol, drugs, self abuse (e.g. sport) and abuse of others (e.g. politics) to fill the gap.

I was on the inward journey but was trying to do it the outward way and it didn't work. It never does. It gradually dawned that it was up to me to fill that large and aching hole, to find a new way to value and appreciate myself. With the help of workshops (some for men only and some for all three sexes), counseling, good friends and my own inner determination and processes, I learned to walk the inner road the inner way and, piece by piece, the hole was filled. It wasn't entirely without pain but as I grew to know my essence (without the trap of trappings) I began to love the guy I am - perfect in my imperfections.

And, strangely, as the inner hole began to lessen, the outer lack also lessened. Business, job opportunities, new friends and a beautiful partner (who turned herself into a wife) all turned up in their unexpected ways.

Then, another lesson was learned: As I had walked the inner journey, I had learned its language - a language previously unknown to me. In this language I wrote a poem to my father. I then wrote a 4-page letter to him, listing the things I was thankful to have learned from him, and other epistles asking for a greater connection and telling of my love for him. He disappeared. He would call in and see my children and ex-wife but not me (same town). He wouldn't write. When I phoned him, the phone would be quickly handed over to Mum. I was sad and I was angry. At the moment I really reached out, he wasn't there. He ran.

Then, in an inspirational moment, I wrote him a letter in the old language, telling of my new car, my job and the things I had been doing. He replied in two days! Yes, I realized, he understands the language of the outer journey (of doing things) very well for he's been on it for nearly seventy years. But that language of the inner journey (of feeling things) is foreign to him; it frightens him for the inner journey is one he's chosen not to take.

His love for me and his wish for a stronger bond is equal to mine - we simply express our sentiments in the languages we know. I had started on both inner and outer journeys (we never really complete these journeys) and had become bilingual and so it was up to me to speak my father's language - he could never speak mine. Only our language kept us apart and when we spoke the same, I found we had the same needs and feelings.

And in his language, he told me how he hated being retired and having nothing to do. He had no purpose. He was nothing. He knew not how to fill his hole.

As our Papatuanuku (Mother Earth) breathes in and out with her seasons and tides, so we must breathe in and out with our seasons, accept our tides of movement and stillness, times of inner growth and times of outer growth, on our way back home.

There's no-one else out there to fill your holes but if you're feeling a little empty, take a deep breath, ask within for the thing that most stirs you now. And behold! Your next journey could be right there, before your very eyes!

MOTLOFOHIFS

From the stories I hear, there are a lot of men out there, "looking for their feminine side". But, like the stories of mythical beasts, the characters have yet to appear before me. Like the unicorn and the dragon, the stories persist but the beasts resist. And so the stories of the motlofohifs (man out there looking for his feminine side) continue and grow and the mythical motlofohifs remain hidden in their mountaintop lairs. And I'm wondering what it's all about:

1. Who started the stories?
2. Why did they start them? and
3. Why do the stories persist?

In all the groups and workshops we run for men, I have never found a motlofohifs. And, amongst all the other men I've met, none has turned out to be a motlofohifs - which is a huge relief!

When the stories started, I thought I should become a motlofohifs and I thought about it deeply. Well, I tried to but I really didn't know what I was supposed to be thinking about. Then, I thought I must be stupid or insensitive or something, for there were so many motlofohifs's out there, just doing it. They were doing it without any training so it must, therefore, be some innate ability all men were born with - all except me.

So now I was into guilt and stupidity.

The other thing was that I just couldn't be bothered - there were just too many other things to experience - things to do, places to go. So laziness was heaped onto guilt and stupidity. Then, somewhere in the long ago, the sun rose and, with a blinding revelation, I realized that I had never met a motlofohifs, and I knew a huge number and variety of men. So where were the motlofohifs's?

Eventually, I was able to admit to myself (quite without guilt) that I couldn't be bothered looking for my feminine side and even if I tried it would be pointless - if I bumped into it I wouldn't recognize it:

"Ouch!"

"Oh, I'm sorry. I'm your feminine side."

"Well, that hurt! Whoever you are, go away."

And in that revelation, I realized I didn't have a feminine side. I didn't have a masculine side. All I had was me.

It's a bit like one of the guys I met in a workshop who, in a blinding revelation, realized that he was not a homosexual man but a man who was homosexual. A subtle difference, you may think. He realized that, by putting "homosexual" first, he was putting himself, firstly, into the "homosexual" box and, within that, he was one of the homosexual men. By turning it around he was putting himself into the larger box (called "men") first and, within that, those who were homosexual. He was no less homosexual but, in that turn of phrase, realized his connection with all other men, not just homosexual ones. Apart from his sexual preferences, he had the same upbringing, feelings, dreams and ambitions as all other men.

As I arrived in this world, I knew nothing of myself. I learned what I was from what others identified me as. The first question my parents asked was, "Is it a boy or a girl?" I became a male and that's what I was. My male appendages put me in a box and my training, from then, was the training and expectations of all of those in my box. The other half of the population had different training. What I was, in fact, was a human with male appendages. I am now a human with male appendages, training and expectations and all of those have a bearing on my male mind. The truth and the joy is that, as I realize that I am a human with male bits (and not just a male) I can identify with all humans - I have the same dreams, feelings and desires as the whole human population - not just half of it. I am a complete human and do not need to go looking for any missing bits – feminine or otherwise.

Then, just when you know you know it all, the universe taps you on the shoulder and says, "Not yet, Jose!" – I wrote this article on Tuesday morning and that very same night, at our men's group, one of the men told us how he had met his feminine side! This experience was very powerful for him and he wished he had met "her" before as "she" would have helped him make better decisions in the past. Later, he found that his wife had met her masculine side many years before and had even conversed with "him". She even had a name for him. So, having met a motlofohifs, I find he is also a vodescadm (very ordinary down-to-earth, successful, caring and decent man) and in a blinding revelation, I realized that there may be more than one way to attain the sainthood that I am destined for. Maybe, if I keep my options (and mind) open, I might have more blinding revelations – there seem to have been a lot around lately …

The Ancient Traveller

C
I am the ancient traveller,
   F
And I see what can't be seen,
  G
Through the veils of your mind,
  Am
And the glories of your dreams,

I walk in silent shadow-lands,
In the memories you recall,
Through distant future visions,
And the prophesies that fall.

Chorus:
G   F   Am
I'm an Ancient Travelling Man
I'm an Ancient Travelling Man

You think you are a hidin',
Behind the wall of your fears,
Puttin' on the mask of a man,
Who's been tough for all these years,

You think no one can see,
The deep loneliness inside,
The rising tears that will not stop,

And the emptiness you hide.

I'm an Ancient Travelling Man
I'm an Ancient Travelling Man

But I wander in the places,
You'd think I'd never be,
I know just what you're thinkin',
'Cause you're a troubled man like me,
You reach out for a friend,
And they aren't even there,
Then you wonder, "what's the point?",
No one even cares.

You're an Ancient Travelling Man
You're an Ancient Travelling Man

You try to help a cripple,
Up off his withered knees,
And he whacks you straight back down,
As quickly as you please,

You stand up for yourself,
And the things you hold true,
Then they shoot you down in jest,
Long before you are through.

You're an Ancient Travelling Man
You're an Ancient Travelling Man

I am the ancient traveller,
And I see that you aren't free,
To be the person that you dream,
And you're a lot like me.

We're Ancient Travelling Men
We're Ancient Travelling Men
We're Ancient Travelling Men

Womanly Ways

Experiencing life as a woman for a week gave me new insights into humans – male and female. In the *Aladdin* pantomime I sang, danced and acted the part of Widow Twankey, Aladdin's mother – an over-dressed and over-the-top sort of woman. To take on this persona I had to learn about walking, running and dancing in high-heeled shoes and about pantyhose, doing clothes up at the back and other accoutrements – handbags, make-up, finger-nail polish, hair (wig) do's, earrings, scarves, rings, bangles, necklaces, seven different costumes and ten costume changes. It was exhausting but great fun and I learned many things.

One thing I learned was that women have to think further ahead than men when their bladder calls!

Another thing I learned was that there are so many accoutrements (listed above) to remember before going out. As I mentioned these things to women they all replied, "Now you know what we have to put up with!" In their minds it is men's fault (or expectations) that women have to put so many unnecessary, expensive and time-consuming things on.

I was astounded at this belief and would ask, "So you think it's my fault that you have to wear uncomfortable shoes, lipstick, mascara, earrings and all the other female fittings?"

"Well no," they would answer, "but it's what men expect us to wear."

Puzzled, I'd ask them to tell me:

Which man ever told them they had to wear high-heels?

Which man ever told them to paint their nails?

Which man ever told them they were more beautiful with lipstick on?

Which man ever told them that hair dye or a perm adds to their beauty?

Which man ever told them they had to pull their eyebrows out?

None of the women could give me the names of any men who had insisted on any of their accoutrements and yet it was men telling them that they had to endure the wearing of these things. When I pointed out this inconsistency they merely shrugged and stuck to their statement that it was all men's fault.

I don't know of any man who insists on women wearing "beauty aids" and I know several men who find lipstick unpleasant to kiss and powder and foundation cream a turn-off. Many men express admiration for women who spend very little time in the bathroom and my strong feeling is that many men would rejoice if all cosmetics were taken off the market. Of course it is important to pamper ourselves and to do that which makes us feel better about ourselves, but to be doing things on the misunderstanding that others expect it seems to be sheer folly and a great sadness.

So, where do women get the idea that men want them to plaster their bodies with paint and to wear uncomfortable clothes and ornaments? Maybe it is the men in the fashion industry they should really blame. But there and are also many women in that industry (Estée Lauder and Helena Rubenstein, to name two) and, without excusing men, let's see where the blame really lies.

If you don't feel comfortable with yourself, you'll try to do something to improve your feeling. So what do you do? You find other people who seem to be happy and comfortable with themselves and you emulate them. So who are the happiest looking people? The most obvious answer is the skinny models with high cheekbones, bee-stung lips, no breasts or bum, huge smiles, lots of money and lashings of make-up. These models also have very romantic lives (we're told in the gossip columns) and so men must like what they've got – lots of make-up and abnormally thin bodies. So you try to look like them to feel like them … men flock to the models and so they'll flock to you when you have what they've got … so it becomes the current truth that this is what men demand, while men are totally unaware of the imaginary demands they're placing on their women friends.

The British medical journal Lancet recently reported that one in 250 teenage girls is developing symptoms of anorexia, 48 million American women are on a diet and so are 30% of the female population in Australia. Anita Roddick (Owner of The Body Shop and author of Business As Unusual) says that the current generation is the most advertising-literate, media-wise, image-saturated generation there has ever been. The average 35-year-old woman will have seen at least 150,000 advertisements in her lifetime and is likely to feel dissatisfied with herself as a result.

It's very easy to be blaming the anonymous people in the advertising industry but blaming them will not solve the problem. The problem will only be solved when we take personal responsibility for it. Also, I suspect, communicating with each other (you know, real humans) rather than the Twisted View (TV) box, would help. Wouldn't that save a lot of heartache, pain and inconvenience?

Where Are You Looking?

One of the current activities (obsessions? fads?) is the search for the feminine side or for the Goddess and it's a very strong urge within many to do this. Whole books (and even magazine columns!) have been written about this phenomenon and I'm feeling a little left behind - I don't have the urge to do these things and some people are so far ahead of me in the search, I know I'll never catch up. I wish someone would tell me what the fuss is all about for, as a really ordinary bloke, I can't see the point of it.

From what I can gather, it is generally women who are looking for their Goddess and it's men looking for their feminine side. Again, I've got it all wrong as I've found my Goddess (the lady I live with) and the search was well worth it - she even gets burnt offerings for breakfast, sometimes! When I go looking for my feminine side I can't find one. When I cuddle my daughter, listen to a friend's pain or cry at the movies, I do not feel more feminine. I feel really good. I feel really me. When my son takes me for a hair-raising ride in his hot car, when I chop the fire-wood or ski at break-neck speed, I do not feel more masculine. I feel really good. I feel really me. And that's all I'm really looking for - more of Who I Really Am.

I cannot cut myself up into identifiable pieces and label them "feminine" or "masculine" or any other word. The labels mean nothing. They are simply "me" and that's all I'm looking for. Having found another ability or feeling that's "me", I simply like to honour it and learn to express it better. There must be something lacking in me but I know I'm not the only non-seeker. As a co-facilitator of men's groups and workshops, I have yet to meet a man "looking for his feminine side". And as a facilitator of workshops to help people (of all three sexes) find their passion, their reason for being here, I can't find anyone looking for their female or Goddess bits. All they seem to be looking for is more of Who They Really Are. You see, to me (simple as I am), those looking for their Goddess or feminine side seem to be saying to themselves, "There's a part of me that's missing and I must search for it, bring it back and become more whole". They feel that a bit of them has fallen off and it must be found and reattached. The people I come across are saying something quite different: "There's creativity, talents and feelings within and I want to uncover them, realize them, release them to become my greatest potential - become more whole".

If we have a dirty windscreen or dirty water, we don't clean or purify them by addition but by subtraction, by taking away the dirt, the murkiness and impurities. Like the water, our essence is that of absolute purity, total completeness, and needs no additions. Polluted water is absolutely pure and nothing is missing - there is just the presence of non-water. Take away the non-you and you have all that you can become. There is nothing missing, there is just murkiness, just unawareness of Who Really You Are. Clean your windscreen and smile at the wonder of yourself.

Another thing I often hear nowadays is people searching for wholeness, for oneness. Sometimes it's the same people looking for their female bits. If there is only oneness, how can you be looking for any other? This idea of oneness is one to be embraced if we are talking about personal responsibility to ourselves, our fellows and our universe. The fact that every move I make is felt throughout the entire universe creates a great feeling of reverence for all that is, including me. However, I find myself whispering to myself, "Be careful of this oneness thing. There is oneness, but there is also other". And I look at myself a little strangely, wondering at my contradictory nature. What my wise self is saying, I realize, is that we should not become myopic about this oneness - we should embrace it but we should also be aware of the diversity within that oneness.

Many are striving to be the same as everyone else (fashion*, television, magazines, schools) and I say "Please be careful, as oneness does not mean uniformity." Our planet celebrates diversity-within-oneness in nature and let's follow that example - being proud of our uniqueness and the uniqueness of every other. Only then can there be true oneness and cooperation.

And then there's other people saying that this Earth plane's only an illusion, while putting their effort into being in a different illusion. "What's the point?" I wonder. Even if it is an illusion, isn't it the one we've chosen to inhabit? Isn't it the one we're here to master and enjoy; where we'll best learn our lessons. We're not from Mars or Venus or any other place but Earth and it seems that this illusion thing is no more than avoidance and escapism.

Then, of course, there's another band of people waiting for space-ships to beam them up - if that's not escapism, what is? I tend to agree with Carolyn Myss who says that the time for evolution is over and it's now time for involution - to be in the world and not separated from it; to come down from our mountain retreats and isolation to become teachers, business-people, politicians, practitioners, artists or whatever; a time for getting on and being involved in the real world we chose to inhabit.

Yes, there are some challenges but I just love this place and the people I meet. Venus and Mars and other illusions can wait till I've had my fill of this one and that could be quite some time for it's so beautiful here!

Someone said that fashion is for people who have no style.

Fish And Ships In The Night

The preoccupation with finding a soulmate is the last refuge of the lonely and it's also a sign post to our new future.

I have met dozens of people who have been told that a particular person is their soulmate and then, after a flurry of fluttering hearts, the whole relationship crashes for lack of interest or compatibility. No man is an island and, as social creatures, we all need to feel a sense of belonging - to a group and to someone in particular. The greatest punishment imaginable is to be locked in solitude and deprived of all sensual input - the darkened, soundproofed cell with bland food and no human contact is the simplest way to insanity and inconsolable sorrow. Lonely-hearts clubs and dating agencies base their whole existence on this need for human contact, as do many psychics and councillors. The lonely and frightened are prime targets for those who can see easy prey and a fast buck and so the spectre of the soulmate rears it's head in so many New Age magazines, psychic readings and counseling sessions ... and people believe it:

"He's just waiting there for you - you just have some letting go to do ..."

"You're just so close to that wonderful and loving woman you have always dreamed of and, when you connect, the sirens will sound and you'll find such inner peace ..."

No one tells you what "letting go" you need to do or how you'll "connect" so, if you're feeling disempowered (and the most easily preyed upon), you'll sit at home waiting for that magic person to knock on the door and swoop you off on a white charger or, at least, a yellow

Volkswagen. While you're sitting at home casting spells, meditating on friendships and undying love/lust and getting another spiritual counseling or psychic reading, your door remains closed to the world which doesn't even know you exist.

A friend was told that his astrology chart said that he will meet his rest-of-life partner (a black-haired beauty) in the next three months. That was four years ago and he's still sitting inside, watching television, smoking, drinking and hiding from the world. I suggested to him that this black beauty may not know which door to knock on and it may be a good idea to go and at least meet her half way. But no, the astrology chart said that she was just coming round the next corner (in her yellow Volkswagen?) and if it's written in the stars, there is nothing to stop it happening ... there is nothing for him to do but wait and, if she's a little late, have another reading to confirm the revised arrival date ... perhaps the Volkswagen ran out of petrol or needed new tyres or something ... there are always last-minute changes to the galactic plan and we don't want to be doing anything about becoming the gods we are and creating the life we desire.

As the worst cynic around, I know that when an idea becomes popular (like vaccinations are good for you or that multi-level marketing schemes are the quickest way to make easy money) I will immediately believe the opposite. For most people, popularity of an idea is immediate proof that it's right, which is one of the reasons why anorexia is so rampant - someone decided that skinny was beautiful, many people believed it and now young girls fall prey to the popularity of an incredibly stupid idea - an idea that has people actually killing themselves so that they can start to feel like they "fit in" which, as we mentioned before, is one of the strongest driving-forces for all humans. The fashion industry knows this as well as do dating agencies and those giving relationship advice.

For this and many other reasons, I have developed a huge amount of cynicism for the idea of everyone having a soulmate for, on the evidence I have seen thus far, finding a soulmate is a guarantee of a short and unhappy relationship. Whether anyone agrees (or otherwise) with me is not my concern here - my real concern is that people actually start thinking for themselves, become discerning about the advice they receive and about the reasons they want to believe advice that they know is obviously based on greed. God helps those who help themselves and it is not our destiny to be passive pawns in the game of life. Our real and grand destiny (and, indeed, our sacred responsibility) is to be creators and co-creators in the unfolding of the universe as all great people like Mahatma Gandhi, Mother Theresa and Joan of Arc will attest to. None of these people waited for Mercury to be conjunct with Madonna, a "sign" from somewhere or the appearance of a beautiful apparition to take them to where they wanted to go. I would not have spent two months running Free To Be Me courses in the cities, talking at an international conference on HIV/AIDS and in co-facilitating AIDS workshops in the wealthy cities and in the poor rural areas of South Africa in February and March this year and then running courses and seminars in Australia in April if I had been waiting for a sign - I could still be waiting for that sign as I lay on my death-bed and that's no use to anyone.

So, take on all the soulmate beliefs if you like, but don't forget that you also have a part to play in this universe and that if you start to create your own waves and signs, that "soul-mate" could just turn up when you least expect them.

And, whatever I think of the current preoccupation with soul-mates, the term has not turned up by accident and, if we look past the individual's need for companionship, we can discern that the nature of relationships are quickly changing.

The pre-Christ era was the Arian era, exemplified by the ram, an animal that is penned in by others and an animal that follows the mob - an animal that gets its sustenance from being part of the crowd. In this era, artists didn't sign their work, private diaries weren't kept and individual effort and achievements were not celebrated, as were those of the group or the society at large.

Next was the Piscean era, exemplified by two fish swimming in opposite directions. Fish live in the ocean and, with water covering two thirds of the globe, have very few boundaries - there is no limit to where they can go and what they can achieve. Also, the opposing fish signify the fact that we judge ourselves, not from the rules of the mob, but from each individual fish passing by - we judge our house by our neighbour's, we judge our progress by our friends', we judge our salary by our colleagues' and so on. Also, being individual fish, we strive for betterment by ourselves rather than by group action. Jesus, Buddha, Nelson Mandela, Michael Angelo, Billy Joel and any other great person in this era made it alone - there were always disciples, roadies and supporters, but the individual at the centre is the one we revere and remember, not the group or the mob. Also, relationships were founded on individual action to create a family - dad went out to work while mum stayed at home and each played a different part to complete the whole.

We are now entering the Aquarian era, exemplified by the water-carrier. This symbolises the sustenance-giver, the server, for mankind. Service to humanity is the common theme here and our self-judgments are not based on how we fit into our small groups (or mobs) or other individuals (or fish), but on the feeling we have of our place in the universal scheme. This is why so many people are finding it important (more import and than ever before) to find their passion, their reason for being here and, of course, their soulmate. In this era, the water-bearer simply gives to whoever needs their nourishment and knows that to water the desert there needs to be many carriers of many buckets of water. The water-bearer, therefore, knows that they must work with others to achieve their life-mission and, in that, they are searching for a special someone to share their home and their career - not just a piscean ship in the night but (like Paul and Linda McCartney) someone to share their days and nights, work and play... so the currently popular soulmate idea is born. However, as every lonely Aquarian is discovering, that soulmate stays away while there is no attempt to try to find and become their passion and, as every healthy and empowered Aquarian knows, that soulmate just turns up out of the blue when they're focused on becoming the grandest co-creator that they know they're possible of.

So, who's for fish and ships in the night and who's about to carry a bucket?

Who's Counseling Who?

Real men do cry and it takes the strongest of men to ask for help. Choosing to open up requires strength and courage; choosing who to open up to requires care and discernment.

As you know, pills, supplements, medicines, machines, and bodily manipulations provide little (if any) healing. Some of these things cleverly disguise pain for a while, giving the impression of health and some give good temporary relief. True healing only really comes about when a person finds their own source of pain, their reason for it and their gateway through it. This self-discovery process can be aided by relationships, divorce, promotions, redundancies, friends, books, accidents, meditation and all manner of good and bad, big and small experiences. Sometimes (just sometimes) they involve counseling.

Counseling has become the "in" thing to do and there are several reasons:

One reason is that people may have a personal problem they can't resolve or recognize and they will see it reflected in everyone else. Because it is their pain "out there', it is vital for them that it be healed.

Also, other people rather fancy the idea of being the person we all come to for advice and wise counsel - dispensing of advice is a big-money industry. This is only possible in a society where people feel disempowered and feel they need their answers from others. An advice-dispensing counselor will only exacerbate that feeling of powerlessness. The counselor will, of course, feel empowered!

Sometimes (just sometimes) people are incredibly good counselors and are drawn to it by their natural abilities. Most of these people need no training but must endure a course for our certificate-obsessed society. There are 3 types of counselors:

A)   The naturals who need no training,

B)   Those who become good/excellent with training,

C)   Those who will never "make it", no matter how much training they get. These people are especially dangerous when they believe they are A's.

And not all counselors have "Counselor" tattooed across their forehead - they can appear before you as massage therapists, good friends, doctors, lawyers, parents and sometimes (just sometimes) counselor s. So how do you decide who to open your heart to? There are no hard and fast rules but here are some ideas to consider:

How do you feel? Good/excellent counselor s will not be good/excellent for everyone - we all relate differently to others. Listen to your own inner feelings of rightness about the counselor - do you feel safe, comfortable, listened to and understood? It is especially hard to know your true feelings when feeling vulnerable, but if you consciously listen to your gut and/or heart, you will hear the whisperings of your wise self. If it says, "Don't stay" or "Don't open up", then don't. It may be that the counselor is good but just not right for you. A competent counselor will understand this. An incompetent one won't and may resort to persuasion, self-pity or anger. Their reaction, in itself, will tell you much. Whether they're incompetent or just "not you', move on and don't punish yourself more - take great care of your fragile self at this time. You deserve the best.

How do you feel after? If you leave a counselor feeling worse than before you started, think hard before going back. The counseling process can sometimes take a long time and "full recovery" is likely to take more than one session. Also, the process with a good counselor may tap into difficult areas of your life you had forgotten about and sadness, anger and other "negative" feelings may arise. However, the counseling process is also one of empowering you to understand and heal yourself and if you don't walk out feeling a little more aware and empowered, then you've been there to help the counselor's own healing, not vice versa.

The know-it-all: If your counselor says things like:

"I know exactly how you feel",

"I know just what you're going through",

"We've all been through that one",

"That's just like the time when I ..." or

"What you need to do is ..." you know your counselor is both a liar and a non-listener. Nobody walks in your moccasins, sees with your eyes, lives in your body, has your experiences, beliefs, expectations and dreams. Nobody but you knows how you feel - you are unique. You know that when the above things are said that your counselor doesn't know how you feel and you also know that they're not listening to you, but simply to their own feelings and experiences, through your words. That is very disempowering. A good counselor may share a little of themselves but for most (or all) of the time will leave their own "stuff" aside - they're there 100% for you and you must feel that commitment from them.

The fixer: This is, in general, a male trait, but it's not confined to men. Listening is the hardest of things to do and to actually hear what is being said takes a very, very good counselor. The temptation to give advice and fix a friend's/patient's/client's problems is strong (and laudable) but a good counselor will simply listen ... and listen ... and listen ... and prompt your own self-discovery and self-healing. Nobody else walks in your moccasins and nobody knows better than you what is right for you. A counselor may provide ideas, if asked, but they will leave their opinions and prejudices out, giving you space to find your own answers. And that self-discovery process is always more profound, empowering and permanent than the one imposed from others.

An incompetent counselor can do more harm than good and can send you back down the healing path a very long way. There are many excellent counselor s around so don't compromise with those you don't feel right about - you deserve the best.

Now that you've read this article, I know exactly what you're feeling and what you need to do now is ...!

Angry, Depressed Cars

If your car is blowing out blue smoke or it's not starting well, you might take it to a mechanic who will look under the bonnet to find the problem. When he's found the problem, he'll tell you that your car is blowing out blue smoke or not starting well and he will put a condom over the exhaust to stop the smoke or he'll tell you to park it on a hill to help it to start better ... or will he? Most probably, he'll tell you what's causing the blue smoke or bad starting and he'll get in and fix the problem.

So often I hear of people with an anger or depression problem who go to a doctor, psychiatrist, psychologist or counselor who "looks under their bonnet" (for a fee) and then tells them that they have an anger or depression problem. For some reason these people walk away feeling worse. For some reason many people who call themselves professionals do not have the skills and/or interest in doing any more then labeling the problems and then masking them with some sort of medication.

The mistake that many people make is to imagine that anger and depression are feelings – they're not. Anger and depression are learned reactions to negative feelings and they're the outer sign that something is not right inside – they're a demand for change, a passionate wish for something to be different. To express anger and depression takes a lot of energy and the labeling and suppression of this energy won't make it go away – it needs to be acknowledged, addressed and allowed out in a positive way.

The same things trigger anger and depression – feeling lost, embarrassed, belittled, disempowered, disappointed, inadequate, trapped and so on – and it is simply our upbringing and our nature that determine what reaction we choose. Often girls are taught not to be angry and boys are taught not to be sad and so girls learn to express inward and boys learn to express outward.

So what to do about these outer signs of inner pain? Firstly, two things must be recognized:

The first is to understand that the depression or anger is not the problem (though the results can be damaging if not expressed positively) and to go looking a bit deeper.

The second is to acknowledge that the pain or feeling of that moment is probably not new. The pain (say, feeling belittled) may have started forty or fifty years ago and it's been added to on countless other occasions. It is, therefore, unlikely to be swept away and "dealt with" in a five-minute chat or with a psychological laxative, sometimes called an anti-depressant pill. There are often layers of each type of pain and it can take time and patience to "peel the onion" of each of your pains.

Now, what to do? There are as many techniques as there are therapists but some suggestions are:

Name and claim your actions (or reactions) – that which you can name, recognize and own is that which you can release. So, a simple (though often difficult) step is to accept that you (like millions of other people) react in angry and/or depressive ways.

Having named and claimed your behaviour, a next step is to never use the words angry or depressed again. Instead of saying, "I'm angry", say, "I'm feeling belittled" or whatever it is that you're feeling. Instead of saying, "I'm feeling depressed" say, "I'm feeling inadequate". In this way you're actually getting to the root of the problem. And don't cheat – instead of saying angry, some of you will be tempted to say things like pissed-off, annoyed, or wild. Stick to the feeling words and avoid substitutes for angry and depressed.

About half of the population don't actually know how they feel or know how to put words to the feelings that arise. You are not unusual if this is so for you and, in this case, you can start to play with feeling words – say, "I'm feeling disappointed" and if that doesn't work, try "I'm feeling trapped". Keep going with all sorts of feeling words and, suddenly, one will feel right. Each time a feeling arises (negative and positive) try playing with a list of words and, as you do it, you'll get better at identifying your feelings – like anything else, practice makes perfect.

A next step is to recognize that all of the dozens of different feelings arise from one feeling – a feeling of separation or a lack of oneness. When you're in love you feel a oneness with your lover, and when you're in a wonderfully cooperative team, you feel a oneness with your team members. Then, when a difference happens, a feeling of separation arises and that is translated into one of the many feelings that we have labeled. Then, as the negative feeling arises, we take action in the form of anger, depression or some other way. What does this action do to your lover or your team? It creates more separation and so the spiral continues. This is why angry and depressive behaviour are not helpful.

If a person is committed to improving their behaviour, the above ideas will help. However, for the person bearing the brunt of that behaviour, it is important to realize that as the hurts can go back a long way, so can the ingrained behaviour – even with the best of intentions, it can be difficult to act "perfectly", especially in times of stress. There is, of course, no excuse for physical or emotional abuse and walking away from the problem is understandable. However, if you decide to stay and help your friend through it, just know that patience and understanding could be needed!

Who Are You Really?

Some people who know about these things (you know, people like psychologists and writers), tell us that what men most want is to be appreciated and what women most want is to be understood. Because of that, men spend their lives doing things to be appreciated and women spend their lives explaining things so they will be understood. It's a nice, simple theory and it probably explains a lot of things. I really like simple things and, as such, the theory suits me. However, I do wonder if it's all that cut-and-dried. I also wonder if we're so one-dimensional and I really do wonder if men and women are all that different.

Getting a bit theoretical here, one could argue that women want to be understood so that people will appreciate them, appreciate who they are. And, maybe, men want to be appreciated as that shows that people understand them. One could get quite philosophical and talk in circles for hours and not achieve anything ... there I go again, wanting to achieve (do) something - typical man!

There's yet another theory that the only reason we're on this Earth is to Find Out Who We Really Are. It's a theory I quite like. For one thing, it doesn't put people in boxes and make assumptions before we meet them. It also accepts that just as there are differences between men and women, so there are differences between Samoans and Eskimos, between athletes and paraplegics, between pirates and saints, between home-makers and business executives. There are so many differences and to simply see that we are all unique and that we are all different is far more healthy than myopically focusing on one particular difference

– the sexual one. Yes, there are differences between you and me (if you are a woman) but the greatest of those may be because I came from a farming background and you came from the city. Or maybe you were abused and I wasn't. Or maybe you traveled the world and I have been nowhere. Or maybe you like making money and I like making friends. There are so many strands that make the fabric of Who I Really Am that I may never know the fullness of myself. And so for you. And if we don't know the fullness of ourselves, we will never find the complete answer for the differences between us. Every second of our lives has been different and there's a difference for every one of them – absolutely millions of them. To extract one of those differences (the sexual one) and to say the other many million are irrelevant, is to make a mockery of the many strands that created the beautiful tapestry which we are. Of course my male body has created different experiences and feelings for me than your female body has for you, but let us not deny the other differences that have separated us.

The other nice thing about the Finding Out Who You Really Are theory is that it not only recognizes that we are all unique, but that we are also identical. We may all come from different places, attitudes, beliefs, abilities, prejudices and experiences, but we are all going to the same place and to the same dream, in our own unique way. For most of us, it seems, we Find Out Who We Really Are by Finding Out Who We Really Are Not.

We may get involved in work that becomes unpleasant or boring and, from that, discover what is pleasant or even exciting and inspiring.

We may get involved in relationships that leave us feeling disempowered, weak and/or unworthy. This gives us the opportunity to revise the list of things we do want in a relationship. If we take that opportunity, each relationship will be better.

Maybe, like me, you were not allowed to express yourself as a child and, in the ensuing years, strove to be heard. That striving has led me to the place where I now lecture to over a hundred people a week, write words in books and magazines that are read by thousands. If I had not been suppressed, I may not have driven myself so hard to express myself.

Maybe, like me, you were told in a hundred subtle (and not so subtle) ways that you could not sing. Each negative comment on my singing ability (no matter how jokingly made) went like an arrow to my heart – it hurt more than anyone could know. However, the wounded strive harder for healing than do the healthy and with each cry of pain, there would also be a cry of determination from my heart that, one day, I would damned well show them – I would sing! And in the last few months, I have found that voice that I knew was there all along and I have shared it publicly. I do not sing with bitterness or anger for past comments, but with the simple freedom of a bird released from its cage, knowing that its wings would give it flight, even before it tried them out. I have no need to be a famous singer or to make a lot of money out of my new-found ability – my only need is to express another beautiful part of that which is me.

And so this Becoming Who We Really Are leads us on a magical journey – men and women, Samoans and Eskimos, athletes and paraplegics, pirates and saints, home-makers and business executives. Whoever we are, much of the discovery of Who We Really Are has come from Who We've Not Been Allowed To Be. Each arrow to the heart has been a gift of healing, of discovery, on the journey to Who We Really Are, but don't know. The Who We Really Are is already inside and we don't have to go anywhere to find it – the only journey necessary is from the head down to the heart.

What were the arrows that impaled themselves in your being? Which of them still gives you pain? What shadows still follow you in your darkest moments? Somehow, some time, you will find what it takes to embrace those arrows and shadows and, in that embrace, they will become your greatest friends.

You will become your greatest friend.

You will become Who You Really Are.

Speaking Without Words

Words. Funny things really, words. They get in the way but we can't do without them.

Our Neanderthal ancestors, cats, dogs, elephants, dolphins, snakes, spiders and so on, all communicate without words. So words are unique to humans and only humans in recent history.

Without words this book would be blank pages with unconnected pictures. Without them, there would be no publishing – magazines, books and newspapers. There would be no computers. Without words there would be very little entertainment – just silent movies; no songs, no opera, no television, no comedy. Without them there'd be no public relations or advertising, no law system or politics, as we know them today, for communication on a large scale would not be possible.

Life would be simpler and probably more peaceful – there'd be no need for lawmakers and law enforcers. Education and religion would be very different. Our truths would have to come from within for we could not look to the "wise" words of others. We would need to be more attentive of our own inner promptings, of others and our surroundings. We'd need to be more careful of our body language.

Words are so important nowadays that they're seen, by many, to be the answer to all our emotional problems. The idea that we must disclose all our inner "stuff" to the world to heal ourselves, is so ingrained, that anyone who suggests otherwise is seen as a traitor, as a heretic. No one is allowed to suggest that keeping things to yourself could be good for you but, nevertheless, I'm going to suggest it anyway.

One idea in counseling is that you tell someone everything - all your joys, pain, dreams, worries and every other thing - and once all those inner things are turned into words, poof! You're healed! So easy, just tell and heal. That method does work, sometimes, for many people, but it is not the only way. There is no one way to become enlightened, to become healed or to become a better person. Your way is not my way and vice versa. The problem is that the people for whom words are more important are the ones who get heard and so the only truths that are broadcast are those from the word people. The non-word people don't get heard and don't get acknowledged, as if they don't exist. All they hear about is the way of others and they feel pressured to conform to the truth of those who are built differently from them. And the word people wonder why everyone doesn't do things their way (talking, talking, talking ...) for they've never stopped to listen - with different ears – to the truths of the non-word people. Because they only hear with their ears, they're not aware that others are speaking in the silent way, the way without words. To them there is no other truth for they've never known that there's another way to communicate.

For word people, expression is the way they operate and words are their best way of healing and self-improvement. For the non-word people, this is the worst way to sort things out. Let me explain it this way:

When something happens to us, an emotion arises. Someone may tell us something nice and there's a happening in our body – maybe heat in our cheeks, buzzing in our heart or tingling in our toes. Someone may be angry with us and we may experience tightness in our stomach, clenching in our hands or sweating on our forehead. The energy of an outside event starts the motion of energy in our body, which is why we call it emotion – energy in motion. Some may leave it at that and simply experience the emotion.

Others may reflect on that emotion and, in that reflection, the emotions are turned into feelings. "I have heat in my cheeks and so that's what embarrassment feels like" or "I have tightness in my stomach and so that's what fear feels like". To reflect and convert bodily sensations into feelings, we must put words to those sensations. Something is always lost in the translation. Even in the safety of our own minds, there are never the perfect words to explain to ourselves what the emotion was really like.

Then if we tell someone else what the emotion was, the translating loses more of the original reality. For a start, the words are never a complete picture for ourselves and it can feel awkward to pass on this incomplete picture - we know all our emotions can never be conveyed fully and misinterpretation is likely. The next problem is that the listener has hir own language which comes from hir different experiences, upbringing, dreams and biases. Same words mean different things to different people. We know full well that our words will not be fully understood and we then have two remedies:

1. Remain silent and leave our listener with a distorted view of what has gone on, or

2. Explain more fully, knowing that the more words we use, the more distance we have from our original emotion.

If our listener is a word person, they will want more words, totally unaware that adding words is subtracting meaning. They wonder at our silence and tell us we must express ourselves more while we know that more words simply create a larger gulf in understanding.

What to do? We cannot teach our word people how to hear in the language of silence for we must teach them in that language also - they will never hear. We cannot use more words for that creates greater misunderstanding. We can do nothing to bridge the gap. Absolutely nothing. We may become frustrated, angry, withdrawn or whatever but there is still nothing we can do. We cannot become word people for that is not our way. We can only try to adjust, as immigrants in a new land where all is done differently. We must try to learn the new language but it never has the fullness and nuances of the language of our birth and no one in this foreign land knows our birth language.

Speaking our feelings is one way of healing our tortured psyches but it is not the only way.

Words are helpful for some and really unhelpful for others. Please listen to our silences and respect our differences. Who knows what you may hear in the silence. Just try it for a moment ... right now ... shhhh.

Heart Of Nails

There's nothing like a touch of melancholy to drag out the inner poet. In 2001 I was recovering from PMT (or FOF)* in Southport on Australia's Gold Coast, next door to Surfers Paradise – a more beautiful place to patch a leaking heart I cannot imagine.

My income, then, came from helping families recover from their seemingly insurmountable debt crises. It occurred to me, just this morning, that, as I helped them to repair their broken piggy banks, they helped me to repair my broken heart. There is nothing like service to others to take us up and out of our perceived misery.

I'm not sure how I got by on so little sleep but depression does that, I'm told. Though I just wanted to go to sleep and never wake again, never face another sad little day, shutting the eyes and hoping for sleep never worked – sleep seldom came.

So I'd get up, make a coffee and take my stuff out to the balcony and enjoy the 1.00 am or 2.00 am or 3.00 am or 4.00 am (or any other silly am time) view over the bay. Then I'd roll a smoke and start writing.

For some reason, I know this song came at 4.00 am – not sure why I remember that – and I guess it came out of a need to find peace in a distant childhood that knew little of peace. Well, that's what my sad little heart thought on that Southport balcony at 4.00 in the morning as I sipped another coffee, rolled another cigarette and let the words fall from my pen.

There is a reference in the song to Jilly, which is what my father called my mother … because that was her name. So here it is, Heart of Nails:

Am   C
I am a fine carpenter, a hewer of wood,
       G   F
And my graceful creations in mansions have stood
Dm   Am
They talk of the wonder and the peace that they feel,
       G   F   Am
When they see, they touch, they smell, my sculptures so real.

But I am just a man with a heart pierced with nails,
Against the beating and harsh words so ever it rails,
But my father knew nothing 'bout gentle and kind,
And many nails in his heart, if you look there you'll find.

You are a fine lass, oh Jilly me love,
Seein' the beauty I make and we fit hand in glove,
But inside there's a pain that's never to go,
And a leaking from my nails my essence it flows.

You would be a good wife of that I'm so sure,
Oh, Jilly I want you forever and more,
But you wonder and look sad, in the moonlight we stand,
Why you can't come closer and take me like a man.

I want to hug you and smile, it's sweet and it's pain,
I feel your kind heart but the nails press again,
I'd love a sweet house and a family to start,
But I don't know how to not put nails in their heart.

So I carve another piece, graceful curves and how,
Not a nail in the wood would I ever allow,
Wishin' I had a heart like my sculptures of wood,
Never a nail or a pain and I'd love you like I should.

Philip J Bradbury   *101*

Wishin' I had a heart like my sculptures of wood,
Never a nail or a pain and I'd love you like I should.

*For some strange reason, though I'm a New Zealander, I can't help
singing this song with an Irish accent ... probably with a very bad
Irish accent. Maybe it's my ancestors coming out in me, somehow.*

*PMT = Post Marriage Trauma or FOF, as a never-to-be-
married-again friend called it – Fear Of Freedom.

The Shyest Boy In The World

For my first 40 years I was the *World Champion Shy Person*. There were no close contenders for the title; I was the shyest person ever there was. In fact, I was The Original Shy Person, the one whom everyone else learned their shyness from – I was terrified of people, terrified of speaking, terrified of disagreement, terrified of conflict, terrified of upsetting anyone, terrified of upstaging anyone, terrified of looking at people … terrified of the world, really.

I was afraid to speak so I'd mumble so people couldn't understand me so they would ignore me so I would feel insignificant so my confidence shrank so I mumbled less coherently … a pathetic little viscious cycle.

I don't know how or why epiphany moments happen but they do. Perhaps, with 40 years' terror stuffed down inside, there wasn't room for any more and something had to give. Perhaps. I don't really know. What I do know is that, somehow, I realised I'd let all this terror rule my life and, TA DA!, I was no longer a child and I didn't have to obey it any more. I do remember walking shyly down the street, feeling terrified that people were looking at me giggling at my silliness. But giggle I did, at the folly I'd made of my life. That night I lay awake for hours, trying to think of ways to get myself over it. No ideas came, then but, in the morning, it hit me like a wet fish across the forehead – why not be a lecturer, standing in front of people all day, communicating verbally, incessantly, and I'd have to make myself be heard, be understood, be listened to.

Full of the fires of transformation, I marched into the local polytechnic and asked if they needed any accounting lecturers. The receptionist looked at me, silently, for a moment and then burst out laughing. I felt mortified, stupid. Then she explained that the previous lecturer had been fired the previous day and they were desperate for a replacement. She was laughing at the synchronicity of my arrival; not at me.

I met the Head of Department and after a chat, she gave me an A4 piece of paper with a course outline on it and told me to create a 17-week course from that. I was panicked but determined and, the following week, I started teaching. I was terrified for six months, every day and every night. As I stood outside the lecture room before each lesson, I had to wrestle my demons to the floor, walk over them and enter the room. I could so easily have walked away a hundred times.

Slowly, the fear subsided and I got it that I had something to contribute. My confidence grew and I started, also, running business courses at the Chamber of Commerce and personal development courses in New Zealand, South Africa and Australia. For a year I nagged a magazine publisher and, eventually, she gave in and published an article of mine. That article had so much feedback I ended up becoming a columnist for that magazine and several others for around ten years. I became the editor of that magazine and then my wife and I took over and published another one. I wrote and published several books, sang and acted on stage, was in two episodes of the TV serial, *Xena, Warrior Princess*, and I was interviewed on radio and TV.

I had broken out of my shell and there was no going back.

Then I came to the Land of the Shy People … well, I worked for organisations in England where the hottest topic was the weather and people who had worked with each other for 20 years had never visited each others' homes. I was confused by this insularity, this inability to venture an opinion or a holiday to anywhere they'd not previously been. I'd returned to my closed-in childhood all over again!

I had trouble getting jobs in England and it was suggested that I tone down my exuberance … which I didn't see as exuberance at all; I'm just me and others not like me are not-exuberant.

So I wrote a novel about it – *The Last Stand Down* – a man who is all the closed-down men I ever commuted with on the train and tube to London and who I worked with. I'm sure most of them are itching to break out of their shells. In the novel Arthur breaks out but I wonder how many do in real life.

It's a scary and exhilarating experience and neither Arthur nor I can go back – why would we want to?

The Violence Within

We had dinner with my bonus-daughter (yes, bonus-daughter, not step-daughter) and she didn't want to miss the netball finals, so we watched along with her. One of the several reasons we don't watch TV was brought home to me. I saw a team of New Zealanders who had made it to be second best in the world (in the world!) and they were absolutely distraught! While the winning team was crowing, the second place getters all looked ready to slit their wrists.

From what I saw on the screen (and things aren't always as we're shown), not one person of any team went over to congratulate or thank the opposition, the coaches or the referees. None of the coaches did this either. I was greatly saddened that a simple game has become so violent (in terms of personal bitterness) and so lacking in anything approaching wholesome human spirit and I really wonder where compassion, love and fun have gone, especially from sport.

It also served to remind me how violent and uncharitable we have become towards ourselves and our fellow humans. Men are certainly the most frequent (though not the only) perpetrators of physical violence, but both sexes share responsibility for mental violence, or the suppression of spirit. The recent replacement of a man (Rod Deane) with a woman (Theresa Gattung) as head of Telecom , has seen the abandonment of the program that saw hundreds of thousands of dollars going to schools (schools now have to take Telecom products – how many phones does one school need?) and the transfer of that money to legalized violence – rugby. While Theresa is not gouging out an eye or kicking a head, she is as much a part of that violence as are the immediate perpetrators, the other players, the coaches, the spectators and anyone else who supports (in any way) this legalised thuggery.

In the same way, we create the politicians we get, by not allowing them to be human or to make mistakes. While we treat them like automatons that should know better, they act like they do know better, they are unable to admit mistakes and are forced to tell lies to attempt face-saving. The lies they tell us publicly are the lies we tell ourselves inside. The misdemeanours they commit publicly are the ones we do privately. The only difference is that the politicians have the courage to stand up and be counted – the back-row whingers are the same, just more cowardly.

When we deny our humanity, the essential us, we deny the potential that we are and we commit the greatest of all sins – the suppression of spirit. When we deny the fullness of ourselves, we see our reflection in our outer world, in other people. When we allow ourselves to make mistakes, to appear vulnerable, to be human, then our public figures (in politics, business, sport, entertainment and so on) will reflect that back to us. When we give ourselves permission to stuff-up now and again, we allow that in others and we are all free.

There was a time, you may remember, in the Celtic villages, in the Egyptian, Tibetan, Aboriginal, Mayan and many other villages, that we often had what were called games. However, those games (or sport) were very different from that of today. This older type of sport, you'll recall, involved music, dance, oratory, comedy and the whole village (old, young, infirm, strong) participated. This sport was very tiring but everyone could participate at their own level. The really strange thing about this sport was that it was very joyful and everyone won. People were expected to make mistakes and to goof up and that added to the enjoyment. The other weird thing was that it brought us all closer to each other, rather than do our current politics and sport, which create separateness and anger. Perhaps it's time to revive the Village Games again – anyone for a whoop up?

Faced with violence every day, we can feel very powerless and frightened. It is very easy to lay blame and say it is someone else's problem. If the violence has an effect on us, some of it is inside ourselves. Only the totally non-violent person will be unaffected by violence. Someone else may have committed the violent act (and that person must be accountable for their actions) but we are not entirely powerless – there is something we can all do, no matter how distant we are from the incident. If we look inside with absolute honesty (without judgement) we will see that which we do not like in others. And, as we look inside, we will realize the power we have, within, to affect change and to free us all.

Orgasms, Knowing And Belief

Some time, in the previous millennium, I attended a week-long personal development workshop which covered every conceivable aspect of life. It was very uplifting, empowering and was the catalyst for huge positive changes for many participants, including myself. It also developed very deep and strong bonds between us all – bonds that will be life-long.

One of the sessions included a question, from each person, on some aspect of sexuality. The group then discussed each question. My question was, "How many other men are aware of the fact that orgasm does not have to be accompanied by ejaculation, thereby enabling them to have multiple orgasms while making love." None of the men were aware of this. The first man to answer showed his ignorance by talking about premature ejaculation – quite the opposite thing. Another man was totally confused by the question but the facilitator wouldn't let me explain (lots more questions to get through) and so, yet again, the subject got buried.

There is a general misconception that, for a man to have an orgasm, he must ejaculate, and then it's all over. Orgasm does not equal ejaculation and ejaculation does not equal orgasm. Many men experience what they call "very flat orgasms", which are, in fact, ejaculations without orgasm. Orgasm and ejaculation are very different things and the sooner people realize this, the greater will be the sexual satisfaction for both sexes.

It's fairly obvious really, but if a man can orgasm without ejaculating, he can continue love-making for as long as he and his partner like. He can, therefore, have several orgasms and so can his partner. Obviously, you may not want to make love for 3 hours every day, but the opportunity is there for enhanced pleasure.

The other interesting thing in the discussion was that one man was interested to know how to develop this ability but, rather than asking me (a man who had developed it), he asked the facilitator (a woman who knew nothing of this), who facetiously said that she runs workshops on it – again, the opportunity for increased pleasure and connection between lovers was lost.

This scenario happens so often:

There is a man in Whakatane (New Zealand) who has reinvented (Nikola Tesla invented it previously) a motor that runs on the magnetic field of the earth (free energy) and the motor is 137% efficient – it produces more energy than it consumes. When I tell people about this, they are amazed and go on about all the advantages to the planet etc. ... and then return to moaning about car pollution and the cost of petrol and electric power. Not one person has actually said, "Let's do something with this motor, let's produce it, let's market it, let's tell the world about it", which is what the inventor would love. But no, we all exclaim in surprise at this marvelous thing and then immediately pretend that it wasn't mentioned. Perhaps it's too far beyond people's belief systems (despite the fact that Tesla had a Volkswagen going over 90 m.p.h. with one of these motors, in the 1930's) that they just cannot conceive that such a thing exists – despite the physical evidence.

And so it is with this orgasm/ejaculation thing – it's just too far beyond people's belief paradigm, that it just doesn't exist. But exist it does and it's been known, practised and written about for millennia, from the Karma Sutra, to the Tantra, to Steve Biddulph's Manhood book.

And then, you may ask, what school did I go to, to learn this wonderful thing and I reply, "None". I became aware, I knew, I became. As soon as I heard that orgasm and ejaculation were totally different experiences, I knew it was true. As I held that knowing[1] in my mind while making love, the separation started to happen. It didn't happen overnight but it did happen.

Awareness ➔ knowing ➔ practise ➔ actualization.

So I say to you, men and women, nothing is impossible if it's not chained down by your disbelief. Whether we're talking about sexual pleasure, free energy, true democracy, total honesty or anything else, all is possible if you embrace it with knowing. And if you want to turn this knowing into reality, the person theorizing at the front of the classroom may not have your answer. Sometimes, it's a good idea to ask the person who's actually done it ... and sometimes it a good idea to ask the person with the knowing – yourself.

[1] Hope is about hopelessness and if you live in hope, you know it won't ever happen. Belief is the next step and is similar to disbelief – both are hard mental work and require constant exercise in justifying your belief or otherwise. Knowing is the easiest and the surest state – it is simply knowing and nothing needs to be proved or disproved, it simply is. If you can move from hope to belief to knowing, you will notice a huge change in your ability to manifest that which you desire.

The Ages Of Man

The second half of the Bible was written about the life and the truth of a man who lived 2,000 years ago. While the truths are eternal and still relevant today, the structure of our society has changed somewhat!

The changes can be explained by looking at our history from a Tao perspective:

The Green Yang Period was the time of water and best represented by the flood of Noah's time and the 14-year flood during Emperor Wu's reign in China. This was also the time of the ruler/sages – the Tao, or deeper knowledge, was held by these wise rulers (Wu, Moses, Solomon, Tutankhamen etc.) and their wisdom was passed on to their successors. The common people didn't "receive" this wisdom in terms of their own personal enlightenment, empowerment or knowledge. They did benefit, however, by being ruled with wisdom, compassion and justice.

In time, successive rulers began to abuse their power and that abuse continues today at an accelerating rate.

The Red Yang Period (the last 2,000 years) was the time of fire and was marked by earthquakes, volcanoes and continual warfare on a personal, community and national level. During this period, the Tao, the Way or the Great Wisdom, was carried and passed on by sages who were not rulers, but ordinary people – Jesus, Mohammed, Lao Tse, Buddha and so on. Again, the common people were told of the Tao but they tended not to "receive" it or take it on – they would sit at the feet of a great master and from that master they would receive their spiritual sustenance. They could not, generally, become self-empowered or self-sustaining. Again, the Tao was passed from sage to disciple.

Because the Tao was not absorbed by the common people (they believed in it as an outside idea but they didn't become it or own it inside of themselves) it was easy for the power brokers to corrupt the simplicity and truths of the teachings for their own ends. We can see how the Catholic Church has corrupted the simplicity of Jesus' teachings, by creating massive graven images and a very profitable fear-based industry. The same happened in Buddhism where the simplicity of Buddha's truths have been adorned with elaborate and hugely expensive temples, toys and ceremonies. The bastardisation of the words of Mohammed and every other great sage is blatantly evident today. This was only possible because the common people did not "own' these truths – they simply saw them at a distance.

The White Yang Period is that which we are now entering and is represented by the invisible – the wind, internet, intuition, magic and the reconnection of science and religion.

As an aside, the Seneca Indian (Nth. American) say our Earth will go through seven "worlds", each being destroyed by a different energy. The first world was destroyed by ice (the ice ages), the second by water (the great floods, the Green/water Yang Period) and the third by fire (the Red/fire Yang Period) when the planet Maldek was destroyed by nuclear explosions to form the asteroid belt, and the Earth and other planets were bombarded with the fiery debris of those massive explosions.

We can also relate the changes to an astrological perspective. The last 2,000 years were the Piscean age, represented by two fish – separation and duality. During this time we have been separate from God, from our Greater Knowing, from Nature and from our neighbour. Rather than look within for our answers, we have bowed and acquiesced to the "greater" knowing of experts – doctors, lawyers, priests, scientists, television, consultants, advertisers, teachers and leaders. We have gone to war and killed each other for another's truth. We have seen Nature and other people as the enemy and have tried to conquer that which we are not. We have felt lonely and apart and have formed unhealthy alliances – gangs, Ku Klux Klan, lobby groups, political parties, marriages and friendships – to feel a connectedness. By using fear and separation, our leaders have got us to leap over whatever cliff they tell us. Those who are listening to themselves are still in the minority – only about 230,000 people refused to get the new licences. If the rumours are true, the others now have a barcode etched in the bone of their foreheads, from the camera that took their photo - sound something like the last chapter of the Bible? We have been disconnected from our inner truth and we have actively sought that of others. That time is now coming to an end.

In this Aquarian Age, the age of the flow, of oneness, women started listening to themselves before men did. Men are a little behind but are catching up.

As with any change, we will falter and stumble. The first strident calls for women's liberation sent many men running – some in fear and some in anger. Then we were told all men were potential rapists. Men, as fathers and teachers, became afraid of normal human interaction with children, as children were taught about "stranger danger" and that any man is a threat. Then we were told that "girls can do anything", while those in the education system became dismayed at the significant lack of success of boys in school.

No one is trying to hurt anyone else but as we try to adjust to this new way of being and relating, many men are feeling unwelcome and uncomfortable.

We're all on our homeward journey and in our stumbling and pain, we might aid a struggling brother or sister. As we do we'll both move forward with greater strength and ease.

The Fourth World of Separation is over and the Fifth World of Love asks us to become our own masters and to help our neighbours to become theirs. From now on we can only advance if our neighbours do, strengthening that invisible thread that connects us. We're all in this together, this time.

Our Neolithic Roots

Many women will proudly tell you how tough they are, how they can bear pain better than men. They will tell you how, when they get a headache or stomach ache, they'll take an aspirin and carry on, while their men crash into bed for three days and act as if the world's coming to an end.

However, if a man gets punched on the arm there's little reaction while a woman's bruise may last for weeks. And there are men who continue playing sport with a broken nose or rib, and simply shrug it off.

Yes, women have a higher threshold for inner pain while men have a higher tolerance for outer pain, as befits our Neolithic upbringing.

After spending months preparing their weapons, the men would practise with their spears and slingshots, to be ready for the annual mammoth hunt. These practises invariably turned into competitions and this pushed the men to greater strength and accuracy. The hunting was a very physical and, often, painful activity and so the elders of the cave would create body-contact games to toughen up the young men.

While the men developed their outer strength and hardness, the women bore children - with all the inner changes and pains that that meant. Also, when food was short, the men were fed first, for their strength was needed to gather the sparse food. Children were next to be fed and the women last. So women developed inner strength to deal with child bearing, child-birth, menstruation and hunger.

While the men were "out there', competing and hunting, the women were "in there", preparing and nurturing. Though the men worked together during the hunt, they had to compete in their preparation, for it to be successful. For the women's work to be successful, they had to work together, making clothes, food and children. The women's world was, of necessity, cooperative all the time while the men both competed and cooperated.

And, though men don't hunt mammoth any more, we still compete with each other in endurance, speed, throwing things, accuracy and in body-contact sports. We've forgotten why we do these things but there's still a primordial urge to do them. We think we're modern and New Age, but we're just Neanderthals who have gained more toys and modes of expression and who have lost our reason for being and doing.

And, in these competitions on the sports field and the boardroom, we must cooperate as well, to survive. This switching between competition to cooperation can be confusing and many have not fully learned when each is appropriate. When the mammoth is charging, you know exactly what to do, but when the goal is some illusive approval from a fickle and changing audience or boss, the action needed is not quite so clear. We couldn't afford to make mistakes in front of the mammoth and so there was rigorous training and initiation for the young men – today there is none of that and the learning has to be by trial and error. The cost of mistakes today isn't measured in individual lives, at the feet of the mammoth, but can be counted in terms of unemployment, family breakdowns, depression, injuries, diseases and a whole host of emotional, financial and physical costs. The mistakes, today, affect many more people and there must be a better way to learn.

We really haven't advances much at all.

For example, of the tens of thousands of edible plants on our planet, only about 20 are eaten in quantity. Of these, wheat, corn and rice account for half our food intake. Why? These were the foods grown by our Neolithic ancestors, 10,000 years ago. The animals we raise for food are not eaten because they are especially nutritious or delectable, but because they were the ones first domesticated in the Stone Age. Our adventurousness has only been about the peripheral things – never about the basics.

The memory of the cave, igloo, tepee, sod house and the village is with us all and, while our outer trappings have changed, the inner "us" hasn't.

The wonderful thing about our eternal memories is that we haven't forgotten the spirit and activities of the clan, tribe and village. We still retain the knowing of the mentorship, cooperation, respect for and listening to the wise people, initiations into various stages and skill in life, joys of community and burdens of playing our part. Because these memories are so vivid, we can return to those times at will, and that's what we're doing in this "New Age".

The New Age is not about the peripheral (and sometimes misleading and irrelevant) things like crystals, tarot cards, channelings, healings and so on. The New Age is about returning home to who we truly are. It's about reconnecting with our roots, our deep wisdom, the Earth and our fellow humans. In the ebb and flow of the universal breath, we've been exhaling, looking out and being enticed by the clever devices we've reinvented. Now it's time to breathe in, to look at our real and deep needs, to recreate the village or tribe, to decide which technologies serve us well and which don't.

Crystals, tarot cards, channelings, healings and so on may help us along the path but they are not The Path. The Path is us and this "us" has never changed – we've just forgotten some of it.

Whether you wear bear-skins or business suits, feathers or frocks, you're still the same inside. And, if a mammoth turned up in your garden today, you'd know exactly what to do with it, for you've been practising for millennia.

Finding My Feminine Side

As a SNAG (Sensitive New Age Guy/Girl), reading a SEAM (Spiritually Enlightened & Aware Magazine) you may be expecting a FACIMM (Facilitator And Counselor In Men's Matters) to tell you that the Men's Movement is about men finding their feminine side and becoming more whole within themselves. Sorry, I can't tell you that.

The idea seems to be that we start as diverse and incomplete beings who attempt to find their missing bits to become whole and identical to other "whole" beings. That may be the galactic plan but it's not mine. My plan has two differences:

The first is to do with diversity. Because of our diversity, my perception of the Men's Movement will be different from that of many other men and I honour that. That honouring and acceptance of differences is an important part (for me) of our movement. For many men, our meetings and workshops are the only place they feel able to fully express the range of attributes and feelings they have within. They learn that it's O.K. to be Who They Really Are in a safe group environment. From there, they find the confidence to express that fullness and diversity in a world that seems (to them) to expect conformity. There is no superman, no "real man", and no ideal model to work towards. We are all perfect as we are and there is no need to eliminate our differences.

"But", you may say, "There is violence, abuse, depression, suicide, anger, sadness, abandonment and a whole range of other negative things going on in men's lives - and you say that's perfect!"

"No", I reply, "Those things are not perfect. However, those negatives are often there because of the lack of acceptance of Who They Really Are. The boy wants to sing and dad wants him to drive trucks. The boy wants to drive trucks and mum wants him to be a lawyer. The boy likes Cliff Richard and his friends want him to like rap. His friends all own houses and he is happy to rent. He feels a constant battle in balancing the expectations of partner, children, parents, friends, boss, co-workers, bank manager, advertising and society and there is little time left for him. As a protective, survival device, he becomes the expectations of others and, because that is different from Who He Really Is, conflict goes on inside. That conflict must eventually come to the surface and be expressed in some way and so the abuse, depression and so on, may result."

A little explanation here: Abusive behaviour is not acceptable in our groups. However, we do not avoid the issue and a man who has such behaviour is not dishonoured or banned. Such men are in our groups because they want to change their behaviour and we deal with it honestly and squarely. Like the alcoholic who can't be helped until he accepts his alcoholism, so with the abuser. Those in denial of their abuse will not be coming to our groups.

Yesterday, a man who sold alarms to elderly people, told me that he didn't sell alarms but was in the business of helping and caring for the elderly. He thinks he should be doing something "spiritual" and selling alarms is not spiritual, to him. So he tells himself (and others) he is doing caring work. It's one example of the conflict going on in so many men (and women too, probably) who are putting on the mask to suit the supposed expectations of others. The Men's Movement is about taking off the mask, stopping the pretense and being proud of Who We Really Are.

Diversity is encouraged and honoured, as it is in the spiritual world. If it wasn't, we would only need the channeling of one being who could speak on behalf of all the others.

The second difference in my plan is the little matter of my feminine side - I don't have one. When I cuddle my daughter, listen to a friend's pain or cry at the movies, I do not feel more feminine. I feel really good. I feel really me. When my son takes me for a hair-raising ride in his hot car, when I chop the fire-wood or ski at break-neck speed, I do not feel more masculine. I feel really good. I feel really me. And that's all

I'm really looking for - more of Who I Really Am. I cannot cut myself up into identifiable pieces and label them "feminine" or "masculine" or any other word. The labels mean nothing. They are simply "me" and that's all I'm looking for. Having found another ability or feeling that's "me", I simply like to honour it and learn to express it better.

Sound too simple? Well, I guess that's me. The more complexity and diversity I find within, the more simple I become. And the more I can embrace, honour and accept the diversity and complexity of the world, the more simple it becomes. A label-less, boundary-less, simple bloke in a world of diverse oneness. Quite simple really.

Tough on the Outside

I f I had been born a woman I would have opted for eternal virginity – not for fear of sex but for fear of the consequences of sex. When I think of the pain of bearing children and of giving birth, I cringe and I know that forgoing the numerous and varied pleasures of sex would have been preferable to the pain I imagine that women endure as a consequence of having sex – far more preferable.

Women, it seems, can also endure other inner pains (headaches, the flu', gall-stones etc.) with more grace and equanimity than men, who act as if their world's ending if they have the slightest headache or sniffle.

Yet some men enjoy being pummelled in the boxing ring and many continue with sport and other activities with broken bones, torn skin and battered bodies – something most women would consider impossible.

Women seem to bear pain from within while men bear pain from without and, in general, this is where we each live our lives – women in and men out.

Of course there are exceptions and overlaps, but women seem to listen to their inner world and have less trouble articulating their feelings while men listen more to the outer world, being able to read roadmaps and explain machinery better. Women tend to rely more on their feelings and hunches and their evidence often comes from inside – it just feels right. Their male counterparts, however, like their evidence to be outside of them and tangibility (can it be seen, heard, touched etc?) and physicality are the basis on which they make their judgements.

Ask a man what he's looking for in a partner and he'll probably list the desirable body, looks and interests (usually his) that she should have. Ask a woman the same question and her list will contain more emotions and inner qualities that she's looking for.

There are, of course, women in powerful positions (e.g. business and politics) who are more aggressive and less caring than most men and there are many men (often involved in the arts) who are more intuitive and nurturing than most women. Putting people in boxes (e.g. inner and outer ones) is not "real life" and we must always recognise that it is an exercise in simplifying a complicated and diverse world in order to better understand it. Putting people in inner and outer boxes certainly helps to explain why The Freedom To Be You! and other personal development courses are largely attended by women. It is said that some people make their changes when they see the light while others wait till they feel the heat. Because women are usually aware of their inner urges, they are quicker to make necessary changes when change becomes inevitable. Men, on the other hand, generally need a more tangible and, usually, more painful reminder (like a heart attack, redundancy or divorce) to accept that changes must be made.

The inner world always calls first and more gently. If we heed that call we're often ahead of the pack and it can seem quite lonely at times, as many artists and revolutionaries have found. However, the inner urges are always less painful and they are seldom logical but, strangely, if these inner urges are heeded, they tend to take us to the most logical place, albeit on an illogical journey there.

The other world, the outer one, plays tricks, and appearances can be deceptive, as those who thought the world was flat, who thought that plants don't communicate with each other, and who thought the sun was hot, eventually found.

Marilyn Monroe was quoted as saying, "Beauty's only skin deep … so isn't that deep enough, Honey!" and this sentiment would be echoed by many people, men and women, today. That attitude probably explains why so many pay so much for labels and why cosmetics and cosmetic surgery are so much in demand. It probably also accounts for the great loneliness, the feeling of separation, that is felt behind those labels and cosmetic cover-ups – for men and women. New Zealand is a forerunner in this trend, having the highest rate of male suicide (especially among young men) in the world. As we strive to cover ourselves up (or pump ourselves up) with a singular type of beauty that our advertisers deem acceptable, we become separate from the unique and amazing beauty that we are and have.

As we take on the varied expectations of our parents, peers, teachers, advertisers and role models, we take on the outer form of these "pressure groups" around us, but what inner form do we take on? Twenty years ago models weighed 8% less than the average woman – today they are 28% lighter than the average woman. As our young girls try to emulate these paper-clip bodies, what happens inside them? One in every four university-aged women in USA has an eating disorder and a 1995 psychological study found that three minutes spent looking at a fashion magazine caused 70% of women to feel depressed, guilty and shameful – people continue to voluntarily pay these magazines to feel that way!

And, as we enter relationships, the outer appearances are what we focus on – dressing well; acting cool, happy and in control; holding our tongue when we disagree; pretending to like things we don't; bottling up our true feelings and dreams. Then, in a moment of crisis or inspiration our true self pops out and our partner/spouse exclaims, "But I never knew you felt this way" or "I never knew you felt so strongly about that" ... and you've only been married for twenty four years! In that moment of exposing a more vulnerable and inner part, our relationship is enriched and we wonder why we didn't do it years ago ... years of holding on, holding back, denying our deepest feelings and dreams (mainly for fear of ridicule ... or the fear of failure if we try to realise them?) and when we let them out, it is what really connects us with others. When we start being real and open up, so do others and so do relationships and opportunities.

And yet, in the meantime, we skate across the outer surface of life trying to impress people with our looks, clothes, cars, houses, achievements and qualifications when what (some) people really want to know are how you feel and what you dream of. It's not until a relationship, health or work crisis that many people are confronted with their reality, their inner world, and though neither sex is immune from personal traumas, it is usually (though not always) women who deal with them quicker and more effectively, having the ability to "know" and heed the unknowable before it happens.

And, as a man, I know that I don't know what childbirth feels like and, if given the opportunity, I know I'll opt for virginity every time!

No Advice is No Vice

You and I might have the following conversation:

Me: Woe is me! I'm a failure again! My wife and I have just separated.

You: So you're the only person in the world who's ever had a marriage that's ended?

Me: But I'm in my late thirties, very late thirties … actually I'm in my late forties.

You: So it's only younger people who're supposed to have marriage endings?

Me: Well, it's my second marriage.

You: Ah, I get it. Second marriages aren't supposed to end - they're supposed to be the real thing. Is that it?

Me: Well, I should have learned by now.

You: What? You thought you would learn everything by forty and, from there, it's all plain sailing?

Me: Well, I had an eighteen year marriage and then some relationships and I thought I had sorted myself out by then - I really thought my second marriage was the most perfect thing in the world.

You: And married people are happier than single people?

Me: Well, I feel like someone who says they're brilliant at giving up smoking - they've done it many times! I know about ended relationships and how one should spend time alone, reassemble oneself, become whole again but what do I do? Four months later I fall in love again and it all turns to mush in five short weeks and I'm a failure again.

You: A failure or a graduate?

Last year I was asked by someone (Dianne Lang) I'd never met to come to South Africa (a beautiful and dangerous country I'd never been to before) to run empowerment workshops, promote my books and to work with her in her HIV/AIDS program. I persuaded my wife to come along and so I gave up my well-paid job and we busked, ran sausage-sizzles and got sponsors and donations to finance our trip. Then, at the beginning of January, after trying everything, Tina and I decided we couldn't live together any longer. We decided to still do the South African trip together as friends and co-workers and, as Tina was coming back earlier, she would then put the house on the market and everything would be finalised soon after I got back at the end of April.

Living and working closely together for the next two months wasn't perfect but we had an amazing time in South Africa. Tina left for New Zealand and I stayed on in Cape Town to run more workshops and to promote my books. I then went to Australia with the plan to spend two weeks there, running more workshops and promoting books, after which I would return home to finalise our matrimonial stuff and we would go our separate ways. They say that if you want to give God a good laugh, tell him your plans! When I got to Australia I found that I couldn't return to my house in Tauranga. There was no malice involved and I don't know what Tina did or said, but it was set in place to protect her Domestic Purposes Benefit.

Sorry this is a long story but it's simply to explain that, after three months in other peoples' houses, cars and friendship, living out of suitcases in other people's countries, I found myself at a loose end, so to speak. With no job, marriage or house to go back to, I decided to stay in Australia and make a new start. The sea and the mountains of the Gold Coast are beautiful, I knew four people and so why not find a job and make a new start, returning temporarily to New Zealand when the house was sold to pack things and to sign papers.

Then I found that the Gold Coast has the highest unemployment rate in Australia and I didn't have a job yet! And then I fell in love! And it was wonderful and I could forget my troubles for a while and, now that's over, I have more troubles than ever! It seems like I'll never learn and, boy, am I beating myself up for it. I feel like Dianne Lang who said she had trouble with menopause - she had no pauses between her men!

I know that some people are going to judge me harshly for not taking time out, getting my emotions back in order, getting the matters of my marriage settled and doing all the things one should do when there's a "death" in one's life. But, no matter how others judge me, none can be as hard on me as I am on myself.

So, with fear and trepidation, I rang my best mate, Darryl, in Tauranga, about it and all he said was, "Well, how do you feel. And what can I do for you?" No judgement. No advice. No criticism. Just concern for me, my feelings and my needs. I almost cried for the love I have for that man and, in times like this, I realise who my real friends are ... and I'm probably not one of them.

When my first marriage ended I learned much about friendships. Those closest to me were simply there - compassionate, supportive, unable to judge and not needing to advise. I did get advice, however, and I realised that I got the most advice from those I knew less well. Like some inverse mathematical equation, the larger the connection I had with people, the smaller was their advice and judgement.

And you know what? I don't need advice! I don't need judgement for I've got plenty of my own. I'm over forty and I do know something though I've obviously got a lot to learn. I may have done some really stupid things but I do know that what I need right now is true friendships and simple acceptance. And, I've found, I really do have an abundance of those right now and I feel truly blessed. Thank you Darryl and thank you to all you amazing Australians who have just turned up, just been there, just allowed me to be a slightly shaky human who is finding his feet again.

I think of all the times I've given sage advice and then I remember the words of Billy Joel: "Take my advice, I don't need it." If I had only just shut my mouth and listened - there I go, beating myself up again! The fact is that whatever our age or situation, we're all intelligent and insightful beings and, left to our own devices, we'll actually get to where we need to go. Often, in fact, the best advisors are those who don't know what to do and simply ask, "What do you need?" True friends indeed.

Then I remember the words of the racing driver, Mario Andretti, when talking about racing and life: "When I begin to feel I'm in control, I know I'm not going fast enough." Maybe we're actually meant to be taking some risks. Maybe we should all be doing more silly things. Maybe, as Richard Burton said, "Life is not a dress rehearsal - this is it!" Maybe people like Darryl, who has had some major losses in his life (business- and relationship-wise) and has taken some huge risks, has actually got it. Maybe we're not meant to learn anything at all but just experience the fullness that life has to offer. Maybe we're just meant to stay out of control and live the huge lives that Richard Burton, Billy Joel, Mario Andretti and Darryl have lived.

I'm not really sure of anything right now but the above thoughts help to justify the silly things I've done and, boy, does that help me to feel better!

Where's Our Wild Men?

The story is told of Braun, the warrior king, who was eventually decapitated in battle. As his mourning soldiers bent over his severed head, it spoke to them in terms both compassionate and powerful: "Take me from this battlefield, to the places I command, and we'll have adventures you've never believed possible".

Those who chose to take up this strange and uncertain journey were not those who knew not of fear for, as Braun knew, no man has ever been without fear. Those who chose to ride with this forbidding and forgiving head were those who had the greater courage – the courage to acknowledge their fears – and the will to walk through their fears.

And so this small band of men did carry the head of their beloved king from the battlefield of others, to their battlefields within. During the journey decreed by this body-less head, each and every soldier was called upon to face their own greatest fears. And, yes, many did falter, many did wish to turn back and many did cry out for release from their momentary torment. None was spared the wish of turning back, of giving up and of living against their demons, rather than with them. And so the head of Braun would have granted each and every one his wish, had any man persisted with it. With the chance to turn back that none took, all persisted. When each saw the compassionate and understanding smile of their leader, each determined to be with their sacred task to the end, knowing full well that their beloved leader had stood in their fearful shoes many times before. Each task was done, each adventure surmounted and each and every man was successful in slaying their own personal dragons.

After a number of years spent thus, Braun saw that each man had learned his sacred lesson and was ready to pass it on to others ready to learn. Then, as they approached a river, the head commanded that it be interred in a particular piece of earth, and that it never be disinterred again. If left to lie in peace, it told the men, England would be forever protected.

The head was, of course (such is the perverse curiosity of menfolk), dug up. King Arthur, in committing one of his three indiscretions, moved the head from it's chosen resting place to Salisbury Hill. From that portentous moment, ravens have continued to hover over that empty grave; Braun being the Celtic name for raven. And so Braun never left that spot, though his head was wrested from it and, at a later time, the Tower of London was built upon it. During World War II, Winston Churchill spent hundreds of thousands of pounds on importing ravens to replace those shot and bombed out of their sky above the tower, such is the power of the Braun legend.

Braun is often called the Green Man and, like the sprightly Pan, protects the green upon our Earth. He is oft depicted as a large and hairy man with vines and leaves constituting his verdant body-hair.

Though his body has been severed and his head taken from its final resting place, his spirit lives in every boy and man ever since. We wage wars not from on foot but from behind computer screens, we travel not on horse but in car, we build our towers not of stone but glass and steel, but the changelessness of Braun remains breathing through our bones, our hearts and our dreams.

The desire to go adventuring, to seek out our limits and to find and vanquish our dragons is imbedded in every man born of woman; something only the wisest of women understand. Only the wisest of peoples acknowledge this wild man in every boy and only those connected as closely to the earth as Braun himself, do provide a healthy outlet for this deep need, as did Braun himself. Every earth-listening tribe creates an initiation journey for their young men to test themselves, to grow within and to learn that which they must pass on to younger men – that which cannot be learned from others in books or in talk, but that which must be learned by self-adventuring, fearing, faltering, resurging and succeeding.

Those societies which have stopped listening to the earth, to their young men and to the spirit of Braun, deride the "primitive" initiations of others, while their young men create their own initiations in the void of wise mentorship from older men. These modern initiations are designed (as are the "primitive" ones) to gain the notice of the older men, so that the boys may be accepted into the world of those older men. They certainly attract the notice of older men as they race their cars in the streets, fight in the pubs and challenge their bodies with all manner of poisonous substances. But no older men are saying, "Well done, welcome to the world of men!" No healthy test is set and the boys supervise their own unhealthy initiations.

Consequently, we have younger men marching off to fight the battles of those they'll never meet, for causes they know not of nor care for, into factories, offices and other workplaces their souls cannot abide but which their untamed fears move them to accept. Having had no training, compassion or power from older men who, too, have walked the Red Road to their own fears and fearlessness, they easily fall victim to any cause born of their greatest fear. Having had no initiation into being afraid and courageous, they avoid both and give their spirit to spiritless causes.

With so many boys being raised and educated in a women-only world, there are few (if any) to understand their need for speed, for pain, for challenge and adventure. So few men, nowadays, understand their own wild man within and, in the void, men of every age fall for anything as they've not learned to stand for anything – leastways themselves.

Yet, when a boy finds a wise and powerful older man to mentor him, he stands as a force of love, power and truth, as have Jesus, Nelson Mandela, Abraham Lincoln, Mahatma Gandhi and so many others who had such mentors. They don't conform. They don't fit. They don't actually care that they don't fit or conform. However, having all been led through their own initiations by older men of integrity, they have no choice or desire but to serve all others in need of their learning.

So, where have all the initiations and mentors gone? Where has the spirit of Braun and all other wild men gone? Our suffering and subservient world surely needs you all back.

Shaming Men

At a party at our place, two female friends asked me what I had been up to so I told them: that day I had been counseling a man who had been beaten by his wife, over a period of seven years. Both women giggled at the image of a burly man being beaten by a little woman, and more titters started as others overheard our conversation.

Of course, I could not let the matter rest there so I asked them what reaction they would have had if they'd heard that a man had beaten his wife ... just once. Yes, righteous indignation. "Then," I asked of everyone, "if you ever see a man being slapped by a woman, who do you always assume is in the wrong?"

Then I went on to explain that this room represented society, and titters and giggles were what this man faced every day of his life. He'd reported several of his beatings to the police and the desk sergeants always laughed at him and told him he was a wimp. He'd confided in a mate who reacted the same way. He told his parents and they told him to "grow up and stop making up stories" – stories confirmed by several hospital visits and a final admission by his wife. He felt ashamed in front of his children as their mother assaulted him with fists, feet and a growing array of implements. That shame spread to his children who couldn't tell anybody about it and would never admit it until their mother gave them permission by confessing – for seven long years they held that shame inside.

So, trapped in his private hell of shame, this six-foot car mechanic had nowhere to turn – the whole world was laughing in scorn at his lack of manhood, while he endured physical and emotional abuse from the mother of his children who swung from violence to pleading apologies on a daily basis.

And, of course, you have the question we all have of long-term abuse victims: "Why didn't he leave?" And, like many women who stay in long-term, violent relationships, he had several answers:

1. I kept hoping she'd come right,
2. She didn't mean it … she loves me and is working on her problem,
3. I thought that if I left, the children would become the target of her violence,
4. I thought that she would come after me and it would be worse, or
5. I thought that if I took myself and the children away, she'd come after all of us and it would be worse.

These are all valid reasons and they all elicit sympathetic reactions – poor him, bad her.

What he would never admit to was the real reason … the reason that didn't (in his mind) show him in such a good light. It took a long time for him to trust me and it was only after he realized I already knew the real reason, that he voiced it. He took a deep breath, wiped away the tears and said, "I'm scared of being alone." There, he'd said it – that which he knew but had never admitted to himself – and the void of words between us engulfed him and brought forth another flood of tears. I didn't react as everyone else had and he wasn't used to no reaction, let alone acceptance – acceptance of who he was and acceptance of the truth in which he was living. All he'd ever experienced was derision and shame, from friends, family and authorities alike. For the first time in seven years, there was no reaction … simply love and understanding. Before that moment he knew that the only person who he could communicate with was his wife – between the onslaughts there were shared tasks, memories and dreams. And she knew the truth of the violence. To be a friend to anyone else, and not to be able to share that which consumed every waking thought, was impossible, so he shunned other friendships, choosing aloneness to shame.

Then, you might ask, "Why doesn't a fit man, who is larger than his wife, not hit her back?" The answer is simply that he has been very effectively trained not to. When I was two, my sister was born and, from that moment, I was forbidden to hurt her. I wasn't allowed to retaliate when she hit me and when I hit her, she'd run screaming to Mum and I'd be physically or emotionally punished. Teachers and every other person I grew up with repeated the "boys don't hit girls" mantra. Like me, this man could not physically raise his arm against a female, no matter the provocation. Yes, like me, he'd done plenty of damage to male bodies on the rugby field or in the streets, but no female body could get him to react with anything but affection.

He'd learned society's rules and, in following them, had been ridiculed.

To have left his wife would have meant that he'd be absolutely alone in a world of derision – the connection with someone who was violent was better than none. And so he stayed with her ... until I introduced him to two other beaten and lonely men.

Of course, they're looking for other men in similar circumstances but they're afraid to tell anyone this.

Getting Out Of Love's Way

There is a popular theory that men and women come from different planets and there are those who, having experienced unhappy relationships, might wish we hadn't all got together on this planet!

This popular theory presupposes that all men have the same desires and needs and that all women have the same desires and needs and that these two groups of desires and needs are entirely different, if not mutually exclusive.

Though this theory is immensely popular (gauging by book sales), wide acceptance and popularity do not make a truth. For example, the idea of karmic debts has been widely accepted for centuries but it is not necessarily true. Karmic debt was, in fact, dreamt up by the spiritual power-brokers as a fear-based method of keeping the punters faithful to the faith, in the same way that the Catholic power-brokers invented the idea that we are born in sin, to keep the faithful (and their money) pouring into the confession boxes. The popularity of an idea is no proof of its truth and though our perception is often otherwise, popularity and truth can walk a very different path.

So, let us examine this idea of men and women being from different planets, or different needs-based backgrounds, without the baggage of the popular hoop-la, to see it as it really is.

If the needs and desires of men and women are mutually exclusive, then it is a wonder they didn't all stay on their separate planets, with a very profitable shuttle service between them every second night, aiding the process of procreation and sexual delectation. The fact that separate existence is not the chosen way for most of us must raise the question over our distinctly different needs. Most of us actually prefer to live together, to love together, to work together, to play together and to stay together – there must be something we have in common. Actually, we have much more in common than this needs-based theory implies. In fact, as a needs-based theory, it is only capable of seeing everything in terms of separation, differences and scarcity. A needs-based human sees all the abundance "out there", as separate from the self, and to attain fulfilment (for it's not within) he or she has to go out and get it. However, in order to get whatever it is they need, they will perceive a cost of getting it:

"You want a coffee? That will cost you $3.50."

"You want sex? That will cost you two dinners."

"You want long-term commitment? That will cost you 80% of your freedom."

"You want children? That will cost you your career."

The needs-based person sees that they have to give up something every time they want to fill a need, so they are never full – one thing in and one thing out, one step forward and one step backward. The needs-based person is unable to conceive of miracles, unexpected gifts and unconditional giving, though they are a part of everyday life.

What the needs-based person cannot see, from behind their cost/benefit-tinted glasses, is that love is simply aching to flow, and flow freely. The love between humans is simply there for the taking. It's free. It's simple. It is just there and nothing needs to be done or sacrificed to be in its flow. In fact, any "doing" will stop the flow. Love only flows through the non-doing, and any actions we perform to "create" love will only stifle that which fulfills us.

When I need your love I say (inwardly), "If I do this for you, I will get that from you." I immediately create expectations and, most probably, disappointment, for you are unlikely to give me your love in the way I want it. I might want you to express it by doing the dishes and the vacuuming, while you may like to give unexpected treats and nice surprises. Yet again, I perceive differences and disappointment when I get in the way of your love.

If I can stand aside, get out of my own way and simply say, "I allow your love in," then the natural flow of that which is yearning to happen, will. I don't give anything- I simply allow and accept. You don't give anything – you simply allow and accept. And if we both give up, give in, to the natural flow that's always been there, we don't become fulfilled but simply realise that fulfillment was always there, love was always there and that there really are no differences between us.

Love, friendship, joy, compassion, orgasm, peace, ecstasy, and fulfillment are not that which we need - they are that which we have forgotten. And as we invite them to flow through we are reminded that we were without need and always will be without need. And, as I invite them in, I see that which is within, reflected in the friend and lover I see before me. By simply being me, by not bargaining for love, I realise all that is and, need-less to say, I am fulfilled.

Now, since I bought the groceries this week, could you please do …

Reflecting On Life

The man answered, "Yes, I suppose you're right. I've always thought that we are all here for a purpose, to achieve something and to learn something in this life."

Not a purpose," corrected his teacher, "but many purposes. However, there is one main mission we are here to accomplish and all other purposes will be served in undertaking that mission."

"I guess you are right," said the man, nodding. "But if this mission of mine is so important, why don't I know what it is?"

"But you do know what it is," answered his teacher. "The answers are within your very being, only a thought away. Your great mission is before you and you can see it, if you would only look."

"I can't see a thing and I've looked so hard for so long," the exasperated man said. "I know I need to do something different - a different job, a different place or something else different from what I am doing now. I know I need to change, but what do I change to?"

"What do you dream of?" asked his teacher.

"Everything, absolutely everything," said the man. "That's part of the problem - there are so many choices, so many things I could do. And yet I can't do everything."

"Why not?" asked his teacher.

"Well, you can't do everything," reasoned the man. "You can't travel, be financially successful, have a fantastic and loving partner, a great family, own your own farm, have lots of friends, write books, work when you want to and live to a happy, ripe old age. You can't have it all."

"Why not?" asked his teacher again. "Don't you think you deserve all of that?"

The question stunned him. He'd have to think about that.

"Other people 'have everything', as you put it," continued his teacher. "What makes you so special that you must aim for less than you would be happy with? What is stopping you aiming for the best? Would you be embarrassed or feel guilty if others had less than you?"

Another thoughtful silence. He started feeling awkward and a little annoyed with these questions.

"If this mission is so grand and important to you, then the pursuit of it will give you everything you want," suggested his teacher. "So why not get on with your mission and see."

"Because I don't know what it is," he said, exasperated. "It seems so close, but I just can't see it."

"Perhaps because, for some reason, you don't want to know what it is," his teacher said, evenly.

"Of course I want to know!" the man said, glaring at his teacher.

"As I said, it is only a thought away," continued his teacher, evenly. "Only a whisper of light away from your eyes. So what is it that is blocking the light?"

"Fear," he said immediately, wondering who had put that word in his mouth.

"Fear of what?" asked his teacher.

"I don't know," he said with a sigh. "I didn't even mean to say 'fear'. I don't have anything or anyone to fear."

"Not even yourself?" asked his teacher.

This teacher was starting to ask some pretty stupid questions. He didn't reply.

"What sort of things are there to fear?" asked his teacher, ignoring the glaring looks. "Fear of failure, fear of others' judgements, fear of guilt, fear of losing friends, fear of change .... Which fear is it that blocks your view of your future?"

"I don't know," said the man, quietly. This teacher was relentless and unforgiving, he thought, asking these awkward questions.

"Okay, let's try an exercise," his teacher suggested. "Close your eyes and imagine that you have all of the money and time in the world. You don't have to work, you don't have to do anything. You can buy what you like - just ask and you have. Can you imagine that?"

"It's pretty hard, but I am trying," said the man, smiling.

"Now, on top of all of this wealth and time, you have no commitments," said his teacher. "You have no partner or children or parents or relations or friends or pets or hobbies or anything. All you have is you and no limit as to what you can or cannot do. No fear of upsetting anyone or feeling guilty over any actions you take. Are you getting a picture of what this could be like?"

"I am trying," said the man. "It feels very free, but a bit lonely."

"Now we will bring in some friends," said his teacher, soothingly. "Only these are very special friends. They love you so much that they approve of and encourage you in everything you do. Even when you feel guilty or silly about something you did, they think it is wonderful. Mind you, if you truly want an honest opinion they will give it, but in a very supportive way, and only after you have asked for it. Otherwise, they totally and sincerely approve of all that you are and do. How are you feeling?"

"It is very hard to imagine," said the man. "But that would be brilliant, wouldn't it."

"It gets better," said his teacher, smiling. "Not only do you have total and sincere support from these friends, but they heed your every wish. If you need some time on your own, they have gone in an instant. If you want someone to talk to or have fun with, whoosh! - the right ones are back at the speed of a thought, giving you their love, joy and approval. How is it feeling now?"

"Well, it actually feels pretty good," said the man, happily. "It feels like I can do everything and anything - like I don't have any fears."

"The last step of this little exercise sounds simple, but can be the hardest part. You can do it - just take it slowly and don't force it," said his teacher. "Now, think of all of these marvellous friends, however many there are, and imagine them all as one beautiful, loving person. Have you got that?"

"I think so," said the man, a little puzzled.

"Now imagine that magnificent, loving person with all of that love joy and approval to be yourself," said his teacher, with a smile.

The man opened his eyes, startled.

"What's the point of that?" he asked tersely.

"Mmmm," said his teacher. "I did say that it can take a little time."

"But what are you trying to tell me?" asked the man. "That I am the problem?"

"Not so much a problem," said his teacher. "But if you can love and approve of yourself as much as others do, then everything becomes possible."

"Then I lose the curtains of fear and can see my mission," said the man, coming to his own conclusions.

"Not only see your mission, but have the courage to embark on it." said his teacher.

The man looked away for a minute, thoughtfully. Then he looked back at the friendly face in the mirror.

"Thank you teacher," he said, with a smile.

The Hard Man

Some time ago a Hard Man came to town. He was tall and broad and his shoulders swayed as he walked. He looked grim and there seemed to be sharp edges to all his features - like a lump of rock on the move.

He asked for a beer and his huge rugged hand slapped the coins on the bar. Without looking at anyone he settled on the stool as if he owned it - one elbow on the bar and the other hand on his hip. Some people you just don't look in the eye and this Hard Man was one. So they didn't look and he didn't look - except when one thought the other wasn't. Conversation sort of went back to normal but every movement of the Hard Man attracted furtive nervous looks, like a frightened dog watching his master's whip hand.

"So how y'all today?" came the cherry voice of Idiot Ivan, as he burst in through the bar door, talking to everyone and no-one in particular. Ivan was a bit soft as he acknowledged everyone he came across and was always smiling. He never complained and always said nice things - lived in complete dream-land, really.

"You new in town?" Ivan asked, oblivious to the Hard Man's menacing look. "My name's Ivan. Welcome to our little town. Not big, but it's small and friendly. Yeah, real friendly folks live here. Ask anyone. Friendly and nice. And hot. A drink'd be good. What you're drinking mister? My round. Two more of what he's having, thanks Tom."

The nattering went on without the hard Man having to say a thing and he learned a lot about the town. The other drinkers sniggered into their drinks, felt embarrassed and thought thoughts of Ivan. Like, "fancy just walking up to a complete stranger and making a fool of yourself like that." "Wonder how he can find so much to say." "No wonder they say he's soft in the head." "The new bloke will probably clobber him soon, going on like that." "Must feel a right twit being bombarded with that drivel." And other thoughts like that.

The Hard Man's grim face had softened but he wasn't up to smiling yet - Hard Men don't do that. He was hearing what Ivan was saying but pretending not to listen. And the bloody beer. He was going to have to say thanks or something for that soon.

And soon the beers did turn up. The Hard Man's mind was in a turmoil. He was now indebted to someone he didn't know and was going to have to say something soft like "thanks". How embarrassing. The alternative would have been to say "no" to the beer but you can't do that if you're hard - doesn't look good. He's not a bad bloke, really, this Ivan. Vaccinated with a gramophone needle, but honest and friendly. Couldn't say that to him though. Not stuff like that. "Yea, thanks mate" will do, and leave it at that.

"That's really kind of you, thanks very much," burst out of his mouth unexpectedly in a voice as deep as the Titanic. The shock of letting those words out fairly unnerved him but he went on. "Just thought I might stop for a few days to see what the place is like. If it's alright, I might stay on. Do you know a good place to bunk down?"

This bloody Ivan seemed to have a way of dragging stuff out of you. No one is supposed to know anything about me - ruins the mystery. Anyway, they both got yarning over a couple more beers (with the conflict between the Hard Man's brain and mouth still going on) and they ended up leaving together, with the odd smile breaking out. The Hard Man wasn't keen for anyone to know it, but he ended up staying with Ivan, who lived on his own. In fact, he ended up staying a lot longer than he intended.

There was something about this Ivan bloke, this soft headed, friendly chatter-box that was different. And staying with him made you feel different - softer, quieter. This Ivan just didn't seem to mind whether his visitor was quiet or noisy and he really wasn't scared or awed by him being a Hard Man like other people were. Ivan seemed to see something beyond what others saw on the outside and didn't seem to care whether people were tough, stupid, big, small, kind or nasty.

They were all the same to him. Even when people said horrible things to him he still treated them the same - with a smile and a kind, happy word. He didn't seen any need to fight back or prove a point. A queer sort, really. You couldn't help but like the bloke, in spite of his funny ways.

Without even knowing it, the Hard Man began to soften around the edges - less wrinkles, quieter tread and less angry thoughts. He was still determined to keep up his hardness. He had got used to the effect it had on people - a bit of fear, a bit of awe - and he wasn't going to lose that. However, no matter how hard he tried, the softness still crept in uninvited and unexpected at times. He might smile or pat Ivan on the shoulder or say something nice about a tree or an animal. Then, realising what he had done, would blush, curse inwardly and put the hard mask back on. Those times were bloody annoying and seemed to be getting worse. A bit of a worry.

As it happened, Ivan was able to find him a job. Not the physical sort of job he was used to but it wasn't going to be for long. Apart from being soft sort of work, being a storeman meant that he had to be different with strangers. Sort of ... well ... nice. If you told a customer to bugger off they did and you lost your job. Not good all round.

The thought of having to be nice to strangers and smile at them scared the hell out of him. But after a bit of practice - partly with Ivan - he was amazed at how easy it was. More amazing was peoples' reactions. When you were nice to them they were nice back. They acted as if .... well .... they wanted to be your friend. Funny things, people. Then they would want to tell you all sorts of personal things about their families, jobs and interests and so on. The Hard Man got very embarrassed at some of this and would be busy, head down, writing an invoice or something. He would grunt every now and then, not knowing what to do or what to say.

Watching Ivan helped and he would practice doing what Ivan did and then it would get worse because they would ask him questions about himself or even, once or twice, they would invite him around for a cup of tea. No-one had ever been interested in what the Hard Man did or thought and, certainly, no-one ever had invited him to their house. It all became pretty damned confusing and scary.

He kept intending to look for a proper job but never quite got around to it. After about a year he thought, "Bugger it, I'll go and visit someone. Can't be that scary."

So, the next invitation he got, he accepted. He took Ivan along to help with the conversation - don't want to run out, you know. He spent hours patting his hair and checking his finger-nails and then (with his stomach in his throat) took Ivan along. Or did Ivan take him?

He somehow survived and sort of enjoyed it. Bit scary though. The next few times he took Ivan (Ivan needed the company) and then he finally plucked up the courage to go it alone. Whew, this was tougher than being tough.

He eventually reckoned he was quite good at this social stuff and made a few friends. Just when he thought it was starting to get easy, bang! Another bombshell. He was asked to be a representative for the company. You know - travelling around, sorting out problems, keeping up supplies and meeting more strangers. But Hard Men don't say "no", so he went out with another representative for two weeks and was then left on his own. Actually, thinking about it was worse than doing it. The new strangers were all like the old ones. You be friendly and smile and they do the same back.

To cut a long story short, he did very well at that job and got other promotions later on. He even started meeting women and that was .... well .... terrifying. Change of underwear every ten minutes. Anyway, he learned how to cope and even ended up getting married and having a family.

Obviously, he had left Ivan's house a while back but they were always the best of friends.

Then one day the Hard Man left town. Only, this Hard Man was weightless and invisible. The body he walked out of then went back to its original name, Peter.

The funny thing was that Peter, who had kept the Hard Man around him for protection, found that after the Hard Man had left, he felt more secure than ever before.

Little Bear

Reining in his sweating pony at the edge of the cliff, Little Bear surveyed the massive plain below, with the meandering river quietly flowing through it. He smiled at the sight of the huge herd of bison, as they contentedly grazed the long, brown grass. The sun beat down on his young body and he breathed in the heat and savoured the clear, blue sky as his pony dropped its head to munch on the scattered tufts of the stringy rock-grass. This sight and feeling he had experienced many times before and the aloneness in this wide and quiet place never failed to give him that special feeling, the feeling of complete insignificance and greatness. He was but a speck in this magnificent landscape and yet he was a part of the grandeur of it all.

He could feel his heart become the openness of the plain, touching and nurturing all who came to him. He could become the bison and that quiet strength filled him with a peace he got from nowhere else. He became the hard, craggy cliffs, the softly waving grass and the lazily wandering river. He felt the giving and receiving of so much abundance from this huge space and he was all of it, and in awe of it from his small body astride the pony atop the cliff. An eagle soared along the cliff edge, passing within two wingspans, and he felt as that eagle - powerful, alert and relaxed - to see the whole world at a glance and every minute detail in it at the same time. He needed nobody, nothing, for he was all there was. He needed no talking, singing or chanting, for the silence spoke to him louder than any other sound he knew.

He dismounted from his pony and walked away from the sound of its munching and in that deafening silence he became all of the answers he ever needed. He had no question, this time, and simply listened to the wisdom on the wind. As he listened he began to feel uneasy. In the past, the silence had always given him hope and cleared any confusion around him. The stories he heard from the silence that he could share with the tribe (those that weren't too personal) were always listened to and acted on by the elders, for they respected the wisdom of that silence and the purity of Little Bear's retelling. It might tell of freezing winters or dry summers, but it always gave a way of dealing with them.

This time, though, there was no helpful advice but only the story of when another tribe of paler skins came to this land - the land his tribe nurtured, revered and loved. This story could have been of a distant past or a far off future, he knew not when, but he knew he should listen, despite his wanting to shut it out of his mind. As he tried to relax and listen, he saw, in his mind, the valley covered with the carcasses of hundreds of dead bison and through it galloped men with sticks that spoke loudly as the bison fell. A straight line was drawn through the valley, with many men sweating along it. Then a strange box rolled along this line, carrying many more people who got out at different places and hammered wooden pegs into the ground. Wooden tents emerged from the ground, some surrounded by large wooden fences, and as they grew and multiplied, the surrounding forest shrank. Rings of sticks and shiny rope covered the land and new animals, smaller than bison, were kept in them and chased around by this new tribe. The grass withered and died, as did the river and its fish.

Then he heard much shouting and argument in a language that wasn't his own. An anger he wasn't used to, filled his shaking body. He wanted the silence to stop its story but it carried on relentlessly. His respect for the silence made him stay and listen. He also waited for some hope, some reason for the story and the good that would come of it. But no good came, just more confusing pictures.

This anger, he could see, spread across the wide land like wildfire, as fast as the dust storms whipped up the soil where the grass and trees had been. And, before this anger, this strength without a soul, he saw people, his people, running from burning tents, from frightened and dying people and horses. He felt he could take no more and the silence finished its story, became silent.

As he crouched on the ground, head in hands, he asked for a sign or reason for the story. He lifted his head to the horizon and saw the far edge of the bison herd begin to move toward him. At first he couldn't see them but soon he saw men and horses chasing the bison. He couldn't see the talking sticks but soon heard their loudness and saw falling bison. With a startling realization he knew the story wasn't of another time but this one. Rooted to the spot, paralyzed, he suddenly felt very alone. Forcing his body to respond, he ran to his pony, leapt on and raced back to his tribe.

His grandfather, Old Turtle, was waiting for him on the hill above the tepees which were nestled in the valley below. Little Bear stopped the pony, dismounted and stood before the old man, unable to speak.

"So the time of change has come?" asked his Grandfather. This old man just seemed to know things and Little Bear knew he didn't have to say anything.

"Who are these people? Why do they kill so many bison? Why is the forest going to die? What have we done wrong? Wha…"

"So many questions," interrupted the old man, smiling sadly. "Just as summer turns to autumn, so the wheel of life continues to turn. The season of Man now moves into winter where much must die, to be reborn for the spring to come."

"But we may be chased from this land, we may be killed and our ways gone forever," stammered Little Bear.

"Our ways will never be gone. Our ways are part of this land and the land remembers," said Old Turtle. "When it is time for our ways to return, when the Spring of Man is upon us, the land will remind those here of our ways. The memory of everything you do and think is kept by the Stone People and all we ever need to do is pick up a rock and ask for the remembering. Never fear, nothing is lost."

"But their strength is without soul and it burns everything before it. Nothing is left to carry on," said Little Bear, feeling desperate.

"They have come to this abundant land to learn of the abundance of their souls," counselled Old Turtle. "They do not know of Great Spirit or anything beyond what they see. Not until they have lost all that they can see, will they see those things not seen by the eye. That is their lesson. It will not be an easy one for them and it will also be a time of hardship for us. Great Spirit is asking us how strongly we are able to hold to all that we have learned and we will have many tests."

"There must be a better way to learn these things – something more gentle?" asked the young boy, fearful of the losses that could be.

"For some, there is no other way," said the old man, with a sigh. "Some listen and learn while others believe they know better than Great Spirit. They have to make their own mistakes to learn another way."

"But they're destroying our Mother Earth and all the nourishment she gives us," implored Little Bear. "There will be nothing left for any of us."

"They will learn, they must learn, that after trying to bend and shape Nature, it is really Nature that is bending and shaping them," said the old man, quietly. "That is their lesson."

"And ours is to hold our truth?"

"Yes. We will also learn much from them. There is much we will not like but they think with their heads while we think with our hearts. There is always a balance and their head-thinking will bring much advancement to this land. There will be imbalance and then there will be balance. We will think a little more with our heads and use their advancements while they will start to think with their hearts. That place between our heart and our head is our throat, from which will come a better balance of communication."

"Hmm," said the young man, wondering why people weren't born with that perfect balance.

"Then we wouldn't have anything to learn!" exclaimed Old Turtle, as if reading his thoughts.

Little Bear was quiet - there seemed to be so much to learn.

"What we have talked of," said the old man seriously, "will not be understood by many of our people, and messengers of bad news are not always treated kindly. Would you like me to tell the others of these things to come?"

"Yes please," said Little Bear, with a sigh.

"You have not reached manhood but you are very wise in the ways of men. That wisdom will serve many. It is time for you to go to the place of the Dream People. You know where that is for we have talked of it before."

"Yes," said Little Bear, with a shudder, for he now knew there were great changes ahead for him.

And so the wisdom, the somehow knowing, of an old man saved the life of a young man, as the old man walked down to a certain doom - a doom he had dreamed of several times and was now destined to live in fleshly reality.

Little Bear rode off with a mind closed to any thoughts that might pass. During the hour-long ride he simply thought with his outer senses, enjoying the beauty of the land. In a sheltered and verdant valley he prepared a makeshift stockade for his pony and then made the two hour climb to the cliff-top without pause. He stopped for a moment to survey the world, took off his simple weapons and waterbag and then sat upon the flat rock in a pose he wouldn't move from for four days. He closed his eyes and, as his breathing subsided, the Dream People told him stories of things to come.

Many of their stories were of a smiling and weathered old man with a gentle old lady, surrounded by children and people of many colours. A deep wisdom and compassion emanated from this white-haired couple and they drew in many seeking solace and understanding of their oft-troubled times.

Many of their stories, however, were not so peaceful and with a stoic heart and an unmoving body he observed horrific scenes of burning villages, terrified and bloodied people, killings, starvation, torture and the great loneliness for a young man.

Every so often his body would reach for water but, apart from that, there was no movement from Little Bear as the sun burned his skin, the wind blasted it with sand and the night chilled him to the bone. In stillness, he knew, was the only key to the door of his knowing - the door to his wisdom and survival in a new and tempestuous world. A different person could well have gone insane, but as the Dream People played out their scenes before him he simply observed, without attachment or emotion. To have done otherwise would have meant a lessening of the potential of that which he had to give to his Mother - his Mother Earth and her children.

As the eagles soared above and the squirrels scampered below, this solitary statue of a young man observed scenes of a life yet to be - scenes of horror, fear, loneliness, joy, peace and wisdom - which played before his mind with apparent randomness. And, in spite of the pains that coursed through his body, he stayed alert to the Dream People's gifts of prophecy, somehow knowing the timing of events. Even as a particularly gruesome scene in which he could smell burning flesh, hear screams of terror and see familiar faces, played before his eyes, he remained observant, passive and still. He knew he could do nothing to change events of that moment and that his destiny was now written in a different book from that of his people. Their book had now been completed, shut forever. His new book was just being opened.

The cry of an eagle told of the end of his stillness and with a renewed awareness of his physical world, his body cried mightily in pain. Dehydrated, blistered and with pain in every fibre of his being, he knew not how to begin movement, for even the thought of movement brought spasms of pain. But move he must and from twitch to quiver to movement he brought his exhausted body to kneeling and then to a swaying, standing pose, like a new-born pony, altogether surprised to be up and uncertain of staying there. Then, he bent slowly to retrieve his weapons and waterbag.

"Now, walking," he thought, "Can I do it?" His answer came soon enough as he crashed to the ground and, with jagged flint piercing his body, he rolled haphazardly down the slope. Stopped by a thud into a sapling, he lay panting, bloody and confused, with his tools of survival scattered above. With a determination he hadn't known before, he rose, supported by the sapling, and slowly recovered his meagre possessions.

It took a day of tumbling, recovering and staggering, with trees and rocks claiming parts of his flesh, to reach his pony and the soft green velvet bed of grass. He freed his pony and lay down to sleep.

The sun woke him with a sight he hadn't seen before - his pony was kneeling beside him as if to say, "Get on, I'll carry you now." Obediently he crawled onto its back. It stood up, walked into a nearby stream and tipped him into the water. The freezing mountain stream quickly revived him and he gulped water and floated, with the numbness taking away the pain. He floated to the edge of the stream and picked some overhanging fruit, then rested on the bank. With the restoring of his energy came the pain again. But, with the determination of a young man possessed, he walked back for his waterbag and refilled it from the stream. Now, girded with all his worldly possessions, he mounted his pony from the top of a tree stump and rode towards home.

Out of the forest the sun burned his already blistered body but he knew he must go on. Some time before reaching his village he sensed that he could smell smoke and as he rode over the little hill above his home he saw why. There was nothing left but burned remains and scattered bodies. He slid from his pony and sat and looked and remembered every happy second of his life in that place. For the first time in four days he allowed his feelings to rise as he stared at the ashes that had been his home. The pain in his belly rose and he simply sat as a few tears fell. He couldn't hold the pain in any more and the tears flooded forth as he cried out in anguish. And the pain and the crying wouldn't stop as he yelled to the Great Spirit in anger and confusion. Late the next day he collapsed, curled up and was silent till the morning. The pain was no less but the tears had run dry and he slowly stood up.

He would never forget the pain or the memories and, from the ashes before him, he became a man that day. He did not know he had become a man that day but as Great Bear looked back from a later time, he knew that that was the moment of his becoming a man. A very sad man. A very lonely man. A very strong man. A very wise man. But not a bitter man.

His destiny had been laid before him and he determined to realise it to its fullest. He saw, in those ashes, the fear of people, the powerlessness of people. In an instant he knew that destruction of this kind could only come from people who did not believe in their power, who did not know of their power. In that same instant he knew that he could help create peace and abundance by helping people know of their power and destiny and to help them rise above their feelings of fear and powerlessness. He knew not how to do this thing, but he knew that he could do it.

And so he came to realise the beautiful scenes he had seen, with a beautiful companion, a more peaceful and creative human race and a more contented Mother.

If you enjoyed this book enough to buy one for a friend - or yourself, your best friend - just wave your smart phone over this Quick

Response (QR) Code and you'll be taken to my website at www. philipjbradbury. com

Or, if you want to check out - or buy - the next book in the series, *53 Moments With Fables*, use this QR Code.

About the Author

In New Zealand I experienced life as an accountant, credit manager, company director, shepherd, scrub-cutter, tree pruner, freezing worker, plastics factory worker, saxophonist, army driver, tour bus driver, stage and television actor and singer, builder, lecturer, facilitator for men's groups, reporter, columnist, magazine editor, publisher, writer ...

In South Africa as an AIDS workshop co-facilitator ...

In the Australian bush as a barman, horse and camel trekker and stock-whip teacher ...

In England as a contract accountant, corporate trainer, estate manager, lecturer, singer/songwriter, website editor/writer and freelance writer ...

Now that I'm back in Australia, house renovating, teaching and writing, I'm wondering what's next!

The constant for my wife and I is *A Course in Miracles*, a psychological life-style course in forgiveness. Through it I have found the peace I had always been searching for - the journey to where we have always been.

Philip J Bradbury in social media
Website: www.philipjbradbury.com
Wordpress blogs:
    https://flashfictionfanatic.wordpress.com/
    https://pjbradbury.wordpress.com/
Facebook:
    https://www.facebook.com/AuthorPhilipJBradbury/
Linked In - http://bit.ly/2aTzZMS
About Me: https://about.me/philipbradbury
Amazon: amzn.to/25X0CLb
Google+: http://bit.ly/2bsbpUy
Pininterest: https://au.pinterest.com/bradburywords/
Smashwords: http://bit.ly/2aNjkic
Twitter: https://twitter.com/PhilipJBradbury

Thank you ...

I am able to put intangible ideas into words and Anna, my wife, is able to put them into action; the reason she's such a good life coach. She is my best friend and greatest inspiration and I thank her from the bottom of my beating heart for being there, for loving me and for being that which I wish for myself. Anna edited this book with her razor eye for the details I didn't see. Thank you for seeing that which I cannot ... on so many levels.

I accidantally mey Emily Cooney at the Brisbane Writers Festival. She took on the challenge of turning 10 of my books into e-books and creating a new website. Thank you for your internet/tech saviness and for your bouncerous enthusiasm.

Thanks, too, to my unknown student from Te Puke, New Zealand, who came to one of my business start-up courses, hoping to help her husband start an aviation museum. From the start I knew she was doing it out of obligation, not passion, and then I saw her constantly doodling. It turned out she had a passion for art and soon switched her interest to starting an art school, which she did soon after the end of the course. One of her many doodles is on the front cover. I've forgotten your name, sadly, but please put your hand up if you ever see this book – I'd love to thank you properly.

I am also indebted to *A Course in Miracles* - and all the people I have met through it - for it shows me the way to peace; that way that is both simple and difficult. Forgiveness is simple but it's difficult to do in every second of our lives. I keep trying.

45
Moments
With
Men

Philip J Bradbury

Published by   The Write Site,
Brisbane, Australia

ISBN - 978-1-326-83810-2

Other books by Philip J Bradbury

Non-Fiction
Whose Life Is It Anyway?
The Lawless Way
Change Your Life, Change Your World
The Twelve Week Miracle (with Anna Bradbury)
Understanding Men
Articles of Faith
Conversations on Your Business
Stepping Out Of Debt and Into Financial Freedom

Some-Fiction
Dactionary – the dictionary with attitude
The Meaning of Larf
53 SMILES
97 SMILES
51 Moments With Fables

Fiction
An Olympic Challenge
The Royal Bank of Stories
Circles of Gold
Gerald the Great of Gorokoland

Words in progress - looking for a publisher
37 Moments With Writing
52 Moments With God
64 Moments With Self
27 Moments With Odes
The Last Stand-Down
The Last Accusation
The Last Expulsion
The Kiwi Who Flew

For more information on these books, see
www.philipjbradbury.com